Birth of a Tradition

Tales and Travails from Rural Richville

Robert C. Jones RCJ

Robert C. Jones

A publication of

Eber & Wein Publishing

Pennsylvania

Birth of a Tradition
Tales and Travails from Rural Richville

Copyright © 2016 by Robert C. Jones
Illustrations by Bob Denys

Library of Congress
Cataloging in Publication Data

ISBN 978-1-60880-524-2

Proudly manufactured in the United States of America
by

Eber & Wein Publishing

Pennsylvania

Dedicated to Al Beauleaux—English teacher and mentor—who taught me the meaning of the Walden Pond-Thoreau lifestyle who lived above the noise of travails and technical stress of everyday life: 1948–2013.

I also dedicate this to all those small towns and their citizens who plan and put on festivals that bring out the town's unique heritage and sensory experience.

Illustrations by Bob Denys

The Fiftieth Annual Festival

The last of the parade's floats, the classic cars, and one slime green monster truck drift by the Flaming Grill on Main St. In this rustic, rural community of Richville, the onlookers of this two-and-a-half-hour parade start drifting back toward Billings Gate Park where the Midway once again entertains festival-goers for the next six hours until the close of this once-a-year four-day event.

The community comes together again to host this extravaganza for the fiftieth time, a time when farmers displayed their best produce: chickens, rabbits, cows, and horses to be judged best in show. Children participate in three-legged races, balloon-tossing, pie-eating contests, plus a Little Miss Richville contest.

Each year another sporting event is added to the tournament. With a softball tournament, three-on-three basketball, a pro-soccer demonstration, a horseshoe tournament, frisbee, golf, and Pickleball this year displays the largest venue yet. The ladies of the Richville Auxiliary raffle their biggest quilt ever—a red, white, and blue patriotic quilt of the American flag and a print in the quilt of the bugle, fife, and drum squad from the Revolutionary War. Each night at the quarter mile dirt race track beyond the midway, a different style event takes place. A figure eight race the finale—a one hundred lap quarter mile Run For the Riches of Richville. Each year the purse mushrooms and is now an astounding $20,000 first prize.

Two tents along the midway beckon the festival-goers with a chance to dance, drink, and be merry. The second tent, a VIP tent run by a large chain restaurant, houses large-screen HDTVs, and entrants are enticed to sample their bill of fare from wild wings to shrimp scampi.

While the midway fare is multi-cultural, standard festival offerings such as corn dogs, elephant ears, deep fried Twinkies and pickles are still served amongst Polish kielbasa, Italian sausage, Hungarian goulash, and, new this year, "The real deal deli special"—a reuben sandwich with piles of sauerkraut and a special sauce lopped on top.

Over the years the service clubs of Richville have collected funding for their programs from the proceeds from the entertainment tent and by working from a trailer with their club's name and logo on the side.

Entertainment at the small grandstand seats about five hundred and usually features local musicians. Sometimes, however, regional or national acts such as A Tribute to the Beatles, An Elvis Review, or Do Wop Oldies take the stage. The country sound seems to be the most popular music at the festival.

Many communities around the country have created similar festivals, some lasting a long time and others short-lived. It is a tribute to these towns' fathers who initiate these thematic fairs. Also, many individuals (over three hundred for the Richville festival) lend their expertise and interests to keep this festival going.

Change and updating of venues is necessary to keep these fairs fresh, entertaining, and relevant for all age groups, men and women alike.

Again this year, this small rural community with its Victorian homes, wrap-around porches, picket fences, fruit cellars, and iconic columned porticos succeeded as never before. Fifty years mark a milestone for this endeavor.

Over a half century ago five notables in the community met at this same restaurant then called Cooky's Café to plan and implement the first year of this unique undertaking.

Birth of a Tradition

Planning the First Year of the Festival

During the 1960s is when it began in this small, rural, midwestern, community town of Richville—the arduous task of putting together a festival that would make its mark on the region and serve as testimony to what hard work, community spirit, and the foresight of those towns' leaders could do.

Though it claimed to be spring on the calendar, the temperature was in the forties, the wind blew up a tempest of a storm, and the rain cascaded sideways, pelting the buildings up and down Main Street and saturating the grounds in Billings Gate Park, which would cause Mayor Mervin LeRoy to chew another Tum; his stomach was already upset from the previous night's council meeting when he and the council fired the current city manager.

Residents called the city offices to complain about flooding streets, backed up sewers, and those old chestnut trees (planted seventy years ago) whose limbs were now cracking; three large trees were completely uprooted and traffic was at a standstill on Monroe and Madison avenues in the heart of downtown just off Main Street a few blocks from Cooky's Café.

It appeared the entire town of Richville—(population 5,021 as of 12:30 A.M. this March 25th when baby William Billy Goldbrick 7 lb 8 oz was born to Mary and Stan Goldbrick, owners of the Good 'N' Plenty gift/yarn/bridal and other sundries gift shop on Main Street—was agitated and upset by the nasty disposition of Mother Nature's recent wrath.

After a long winter when a record snowfall blanketed the region, it seemed this tiny rural midwestern town received the bulk of the assault. The county's supply of salt was depleted by mid winter and Richville's tertiary rural roads were left unplowed. The secondary roads were only handled by two of Richville's plow trucks, which broke down it seemed every other trip out of the DPW garage.

The mayor made his way to Cooky's Café for an informal yet important meeting to begin making plans for a yearly festival that would put some identity to this town; make the folks proud to be citizens of Richville; and would add to the commerce of the community and region.

Of course Mary would not attend having just given birth to her fourth baby boy,another future taxpayer.

The other committee members took time from their busy schedule to attend, not knowing and perhaps not trusting what the mayor was up to.

They were already in attendance at the café, sipping Cooky's new Kawa/Columbian spiced coffee and munching on Cooky's special bear claws (more like the size of elephant ears, but thicker and gooey with jelly filling), Cooky's wife Nelly's own homemade concoction.

Reverend Harold Huether of Richville Greater Lutheran United Church begrudgingly started off for the meeting. He was irritated this Monday morning, as he claimed to spend over fifteen hours a week on each sermon and was sacrificing this Monday to begin this arduous task. Yesterday's sermon, "Is there anything gay in a gay marriage?" was not taken to heart by the parishioners, many of whom walked out in the middle of the sermon. Needless to say, his suggestion box overflowed with repugnant comments, some even asking him to resign his post. So much for a departure from the "Bringing in the Sheaves; Do unto others" sermons of the recent past.

Dr. Wm. Duvall PhD, DDS, superintendent of the Richville school system, also broke away from his busy Monday morning schedule to attend. He was deeply upset over the fact that this winter the streets were not plowed early enough, if at all, and were not plowed adequately in the rural farmland community of Richville, resulting in fourteen days of closure for this district so far. The mayor apparently didn't sign a county snow plowing contract by the deadline. The Richville school district now faced the possibility of having more days off due to ice damage and potential floods all over town due to inadequate sewers and drainage problems.

Dr. DuVall, a dentist of ten years, convinced the State Board of Education to keep the DDS on his certificate. For the last twenty years, he served as superintendent of Richville; however, he was tiring of the job and desired employment elsewhere, perhaps at the newly-formed intermediate school system.

The last of the committee members, Rapid Rory Reigns, arrived early at Cooky's to try and convince Cooky to go in on a sure-fire business venture, a franchise selling hamburgers and fries with some kind of rainbow arch in its logo, soon coming to Richville.

"That's a crazy idea," bellowed Cooky. "That will never make a buck, and nobody owning such a business will want to just mass produce burgers and fries—absurd!"

Rapid Rory owned a party store aptly named Rapid Rory's, the town movie cinema he called The Rapid Rialto, the town laundromat The Richville Rapid Cleaners, and half interest in the local golf course, Hickory Stick Glen. He wants the name changed to honor World War II veterans, perhaps Bello Woods or as others suggested The Enola Gay or Battle of the Bulge Greens. This needs to be discussed further.

The city council managed to completely redo all the storefronts along Main Street with a Victorian theme or turn-of-the-century vintage. The mayor wanted more discussions of this topic; the time to apply for this fiscal year elapsed and now the application had to be submitted again next year by June 30th.

Added to this was the discussion of an industrial park possibly coming to Richville to provide jobs and taxes to the community. Again, the mayor hesitated as he wanted, "more study on this important topic."

Rory, the ever-impatient entrepreneur, said to Cooky, "I'll give fifteen more minutes, then I'm outta here—money waits for no man. I have to go chase some greenbacks today. My time is precious."

No sooner had these words been uttered that the mayor The Honorable Mervin LeRoy sauntered into Cooky's.

"Hi, boys. Let's get started; my time is short. This won't take much time. Just get me some tea, light lemon, not any of that new crazy Java of yours and no elephant claws or whatever you call that digestive catastrophe.

"I heard Mary had her baby, boy number four. What a blessing. She and Stan have really spaced their children out— eight, five, three and now baby Billy," said the mayor, now out of breath.

"We'll have four committees for this festival— fund raising and finance, activities, publicity and recruitment, and a business and service club committee." The mayor was now really puffing and gasping for air.

The mayor continued, "Doctor, you take the publicity and recruitment; your word and reputation around town is golden. Rory, you take activities—you always wanted a big parade and a horse race on the track behind the park. Put it together. Reverend, you take fund raising and finance. I always thought you went into the wrong career . . . a *minister* . . . come now, you should have been a CPA. You were able to raise enough money to expand the sanctuary, create an activity hall on the side of the church to make it the largest in the county, *and* still have enough left over to redecorate your minister's house—congrats, Reverend.

"We'll let Mary make contact with area businesses and service clubs and the Chamber. I'll oversee everything. We'll meet next Monday morning, same time same place.

"Think of a name for this festival. Make it a nostalgic one that clicks with everyone young and old. Remember it's not just a fair, but a festival; we are not just about jams and jellies, but tradition. Now get busy.

"By the way, Cooky, your tea is weak and where did you get such a sweet lemon—lemons are tart. See you later, boys." With that the meeting was adjourned—no Roberts Rules of Order here, just a one-way order, up front, to the point, period.

The mayor bolted off to another meeting with the DPW department and to his second office at his barbershop—as the Honorable Mervin LeRoy *was* the town barber—two chairs and the closest shaves in the county.

His shop was next door to the newly-erected Fire Hall of which Mervin (Honorable) was chief (small c) of the volunteer firemen. Maybe next fiscal year would see a paid department. As the town grew, the need for full-time firemen grew. That need and to have a self-sufficient EMS department were needs that needed to be addressed and soon.

So in this small but growing rural town of Richville in the Midwest in this most miserable of early springs fifty one years ago (you guess the year), with each town leader and interested citizens, the idea of a new type of festival had spawned. Where would it lead? Would it unravel before it got off the ground? Would the town "fathers" give up with each having his or her own particular daunting problems? Stay tuned to this perilous human interest story. You have been introduced to this cast of characters, but what of their character? Would there be more citizens stepping forward to add input? What of the political ramifications? Who from the county or state could help?

When will it warm up and dry out in this town? Will there be brighter days ahead when the lilacs, forsythia, daffodils, and tulips bloom? That is a tale for another day.

And life goes on in Richville.

Rapid Rory Reigns

Richville's Entrepreneur par Excellence

Rapid Rory Reigns, Richville's resident entrepreneur par excellence, owned the Rialto Theatre, the town's only theatre; however, it was not making money. It featured past World War II movies and many starring Audie Murphy, a Medal of Honor recipient with whom not many residents were enamored. And Mickey Rooney reels were passe'. The youth of Richville went to these movies to hide in the dark and play make-out games. Rory would occasionally flick the lights on, which annoyed these party animals.

Also, the adults were not thrilled with the bill of fare that ran from John Ford Westerns to Boris Karloff to Charlie Chan.

The prices of popcorn and other goodies were going up, and there were many drafty areas in the cavernous building.

The cost of heat rose beyond the cost of living and inflation.

Ever the businessman, Rory wanted to convert this barn-like structure into a bowling alley. Bowling was becoming a sport (some say a hobby for the ne'er do well) and leagues were sprouting up everywhere.

There was only one other alley in the region, the Bay Roma in Anchorville along Lake Luigi about twenty miles away.

Rory started working on his plan. He had to go to the council to ask for a permit to make the change and then contact a company to install the alleys and machinery. (There was a pro bowler, Wrong foot Lou Campi who owned a company which would meet Rory's challenge in this fledgling business.)

He would be able, if he could wrestle a liquor license from the county pals, to sell certain liquid refreshments. He would form leagues, set up tournaments, and put Richville on the map as more than just a pit stop through a small burg on the way to M19 and M53 up north.

Rory would show the mayor this "ville" didn't need a flowery, pansy, prissy, out-in-the-middle-of-nowhere fru-fru festival concocted to make people feel good about themselves. If people didn't already feel good then no artsy-smartsy four-day event of who knows what would put Richville on any map.

Anyway, if Rory thought about it and wanted to race horses on the track at the far end of Billings Gate Park, he would do it on his own terms, his own way without a fair. He chuckled to himself and chortled, "I'll create an affair for all to remember at this track and bring in thoroughbreds. Maybe even harness racing.

"This town needs more recreation and entertainment venues, not a ridiculous fair, which only lasts four days. We need yearly activities. The big cheeses in the county will recognize Richville as the playground of the region."

Rapid Rory certainly had big ideas, some "Pie in the Sky," some practical. He certainly had a stubborn streak. Rory could be charming or ruthless depending on whom he was dealing with and what the business deal was all about.

He loved his adopted town Richville, but he felt it needed to grow and prosper. His way. Though he hired five employees from the big city to take care of many day-to-day operations, Rory preferred to deal alone with the big decisions.

Time would tell if his many entrepreneurial activities would take flight. Certainly now he was meeting a payroll and providing much-needed (minus the theatre) services to a community he didn't want to see stuck in the mid-twentieth century.

While not normally a joiner—no Rotary club or Chamber for Rory—he realized the need to convince the town fathers of his grandiose plans and schemes.

What is Rory's fate in this fledgling town in the heart of the Midwest?

And life goes on in Richville.

A Name Is Decided upon for the Festival

On April Fool's Day

The week of March 25th ended as it had begun, with the sewers clogged with water and unsavory filth, chestnut tree branches blocking Monroe and Madison streets, and the rural roads mired in sludge-like muck and impassable. School was closed Thursday and Friday and Dr. Wm. DuVall superintendent was enraged. The phone calls to his office lit up the switchboard, but all he could do was hope Mother Nature cooperated and the sun would once again shine down on these roads and permeate this rural midwestern town of Richville.

It was appropriate, the next meeting of the festival committee was Monday April 1st. This time Mary Goldbrick was at Cooky's with baby William Billy. She was just getting back to work at the Good 'N' Plenty gift shop and beginning to order her spring items.

She didn't want to be taken away from the store for long and tried to move the meeting along.

Everyone was in attendance. The main order of business (again no Robert's Rules of Order) was the naming of this new nebulous festival. Names suggested were Bygone Years of Yore (too medieval sounding), Let Freedom in Richville Ring (too patriotic and fourth of July sounding), The Victorian Festival (too simple and locked into one theme), Festival of the Senses Past, Present, and Future (where does Richville fit into this theme?).

It was generally accepted after much discussion the title would be Remembrance of Good Days Past—Richville has Time for You (to be shortened, maybe, at a later date).

The date was set for this great, daunting undertaking—the week after Labor Day.

And life goes on in Richville.

Origin of the Loving Rock in Richville

Most small towns have a large rock placed in a strategic place where citizens may place messages, usually painted on, signifying significant events in the lives of these citizens.

Such a rock was quarried for the citizens of Richville and placed in the middle of Billings Gate Park not far from the town's gazebo.

This rock measured a full seven feet tall and a girth of over eight feet around. Five years ago the subject of a "loving rock" was brought up by the mayor. He was getting tired of hearing of these other villages that had such a rock and their citizens tagged the rock with personal heartfelt messages and significant events, especially students of their local high school around prom time and graduation. The subject of a loving rock was, however, dropped from the agenda these evenings at those council meetings.

Leave it up to the citizens of Richville, especially the Carlotto family who owned the local quarry, to come to the rescue. The sons Billy, Jimmy, and Johnny Carlotto had taken over the rock business from their father Guido who built the business from pebbles (just kidding). But seriously, the story of this family business is but another success in the annals of the history of the many businesses of Richville that have succeeded.

Actually, the quarry was originally a part of the great glacial moraine of the area. Guido's father Gacamo Carlucci bought this land over a hundred years ago. Others began to farm this area as the land was rich, the loam was plentiful, and farms flourished. Prices for wheat, corn, and vegetable crops were high and farm cooperatives, bureaus, and the grange movement also flourished. Carlucci thought rocks were the future for this fledgling area.

Carlucci saw the need to sell rocks for borders and fences around these farm properties. The land he purchased was at the top of a glacial moraine. The elevation sloped 1500 feet to a ridge then dropped another 500 feet to a valley below. The town of Richville grew up in this valley; the farms spread around a central core where stores, a grain elevator, a hotel, and neighborhoods bloomed. The original town father Mervin Leroy's grandfather Melvin put aside a space, a park called Billings Gate Park, for the townspeople to enjoy.

It was left to Billy to find the boulder at the crest of the hill and have it hauled to the park. Jimmy and Johnny and their employees took the old forty-seven-stake truck to the edge of the quarry where the boulder lay encased in mud, other rocks, and plant roots. It took two days to dig up the boulder and transport it to the park.

There would be a dedication ceremony when this boulder was finally placed in the park. Mervin LeRoy, the ever-present entrepreneur/mayor set the date for this moment to dedicate and bless the great Richville Boulder.

The boulder was analyzed to be a conglomeration of types of rock—part granite, mica, pyrite, sandstone, limestone, and other sedimentary types. As the mayor would say in his dedication speech (always a speech): "The variety of stone emblazoned in this rock is emblematic of our town's heritage. The many travelers from various ethnic worlds who came to our area to plant their roots down and raise their families in this greatest of all small towns—Richville...."

The hundred or so residents who came out to the dedication during that rain-soaked spring morning heard the bluster and for the most part thought the speech overstated. The rock remained in place, ready for any message, mostly positive, that would communicate to all who would visit the rock the town's big events and small happenings—birthdays, engagements, weddings, graduations, who loves who, meanderings, and short tomes meant for the town to see.

Now, the Loving Rock has been in place for a few years. Petey Snodgrass Sr., the town scholar, announced his acceptance to MIT: "I will see MIT because of my ACTs, hard work, and political pull of my Uncle Garry also an MIT graduate and owner of a large accounting firm in northeast America.

The birth of many babies have been announced on the rock: Little Susan Dade 3 lbs 4 oz; Mindy Falsam 6 lb 8 oz—healthy baby girl; Rocco Binion 9 lb 10 oz Ceasarian ouch!; Michael William Joshua Bannyon Ryan 10 lb 4 oz—a true blue Irish Catholic.

The typical Justin (*pic of heart with arrow) Shawna; Dirk adores Brianna cropped up; or even Evan + Joe made its way on the rock.

Announcements of plays (local stock theatre), high school musicals, and other entertainment venues showed up.

Occasionally death notices were painted on the rock (i.e., Marv Fisher—the eternal wisher RIP or Al Seeman—the one and only free man bachelor for life RIP).

The rock thus represents a continuing saga of the changes in the community of Richville—the announcements, events, and happenings in the community.

And life goes on.

Families Who Settled in Richville

Their Part Added to the Story

As the weather began to warm, the area farmers began turning over their soil to begin spring planting. The local farm bureau busily aided farmers with new methods of planting and tilling. They gave advice on the rotation of crops—one year wheat, one year soy bean, one year let the ground go fallow.

The Gobbel brothers, Mathew, Mark, Luke, and Mosha, owned the most acreage in the area. While wheat was their staple crop, they started experimenting with a variety of vegetables including broccoli, squash, cauliflower, beans, okra, greens (chard, spinach), peppers, feed corn, and tomatoes (debate raged—fruit or vegetable). They, of course, had the largest roadside stand in the area, spanning early summer through late fall two miles north of town on M19.

Their feed corn silo was the highest in the area and rivaled the height of the Richville water tower (next chapter), which the town fathers and mothers complained about to no end; no building or erected object should surpass the height of the water tower, which supplied potable liquid energy to the town folk at a reasonable rate, clean-filtered and self-sustaining. The tower it seemed grew a life of its own and the town folk claimed it resembled a strange UFO planted right in their own backyard (on stilts of course).

Other families who settled Richville laid claim to other forms of "making a living from the land." The Knudson family—Petr, Petra, and their twins Johnny and Jeanny (fraternal)—came to the area shortly after the Great War. They originally wanted to settle in northern Minnesota but didn't really relish the harsh winters there. Petr (the Pater head of the family) suffered from a debilitating roseola condition whereupon facial and bodily contact with outdoor temperatures of forty degrees or below broke out in painful red blotches and puffy skin rashes. No creams, lotions, homemade remedies, or dermatological intervention helped to alleviate this most foul of Scandinavian conditions.

The bottom line—this family would rather stay here and settle into life in this midwestern location with semi severe winters than face the arctic surges in northern Minnesota with their Scandinavian brethren. Going to a warmer clime was not an option as Petr the "gentleman" of the family only sweated on one side of his body; the complications evident, case closed.

This most gregarious of families—in ingenuity, not in communicative social situations—sought to bring a part of their Scandinavian heritage with them to Richville: that of tree farming with heavy emphasis on the Yule tree.

Over the vast expanse of their land from small seedlings to saplings to now fully grown pines and firs, their acreage abounded with the fruits of their labor. They would provide the citizens of Richville and the town itself a thirty to thirty-five foot evergreen in the town square each holiday season with enough greenery to start the green revolution (which wouldn't begin for another fifty years).

The Knudson family always smelled of a certain pine scent depending on what part of their acreage they were attending to at any given time.

The family started a small gift shop inside their barn number two, built inadvertently too close to the road, but now was easily accessible to the townspeople and passersby just meandering through.

Their way of explaining this error in barn building (Petr was fined for his architectural mistake—no right of deviation was permitted by the town council) was that we just goofed up. The gift shop flourished and their tree farm brought the family, over time, a pile of gold. Kroners.

Petr became a member of all the best business clubs; he started the Chamber of Commerce; was president of the Richville Farm Bureau; and even became a 32nd degree mason.

He was also an original founding member of the Sons of the Viking Mist, a group of Scandinavians who searched their heritage for Viking ancestors and explored the many stories of pillaging and plundering of the Viking era.

Petr, with his red hair and red face (roseola infected skin), pronounced himself to be a distant cousin to Eric the Red; though this tree may have been from a weeping willow long ago, the branches snapped off and progressed through some historical sewage system.

And life goes on in Richville.

The Richville Water Tower

A Monument to the Citizens of Richville

The giant Richville water tower stood majestically in a plot of ground next to the city's Cemetery of Eternal Rest and Enshrinement, a beacon to surrounding rural communities who could only hope to build such a Tower of Power. This one hundred plus feet of super structure—some said the Eiffel Tower with no intended municipal purpose other than to besmirch the Paris landscape—played second fiddle to this super structure. Just ask Petey Snodgrass Sr., the only town historian—truth teller who actually visited Paris, France for the ultimate comparison.

The structure, which held 220,000 gallons of potable filtered water and could be used to aerate area farms and which would filter into the city's plumbing infrastructure at peak hours, would serve as a communal reminder of the value of keeping residents hydrated with safe liquid gold. The parks' water fountains would burst forth spring through late fall with non-toxic, pure, clean, fresh, cold H_2O. Through spring, summer, and fall, many enjoyed the fresh splash of liquid spouting into the oral cavity of life—youth, while riding their Schwinn specials or walking in their new Buster Brown leather uppers; moms pulling their Red Ryder wagons with toddlers in tow; Richville businessmen escaping to the park one noon hour for a brief respite from the duties of commerce. Unlike the fountains of other small towns, the Richville fountains remained steadfast in their pressure. Even Petey Snodgrass Sr.—town historian, intellectual, self-proclaimed cultural/biographical critic and writer of light whimsical verse, pertinent to small towns in rural places, and a visitor to the cultural hot spots of the world, Paris, France among other locations—claimed the Richville water to be pure, fresh, cold, clean, and even medicinal. This last comment references a nearby community's claim that their water had a sulphur quality, a rotten egg, gaseous smell, yet was medicinal when bottled and or sat in in a tub-like environment and relieved aches, pains, and certain arthritic encumbrances.

Petey Snodgrass Sr., the ever-present "doubting Thomas," felt these claims not to be substantiated (as it was a non-biblical reference) and felt this nearby community was exploiting their citizenry and other persons of the regions who may be prone to spending their time and money on such "Tom Foolery."

To just ingest a cool drink of this pure water on a warm or hot day when the sweat glands excrete their liquid excess is enough of a benefit to join the Hallelujah chorus in praise to the Eternal Master on High, or so Petey Snodgrass, the self-proclaimed town scholar of Richville, would utter without hesitation.

This envy may come in many styles and sizes. The town fathers from those other rural entities marveled at this Tower of Babel, a wish from other community members that this water tower would somehow burst, collapse, and drown (not in a real sense) the fleeing public in Richville.

Phil Dickerson, the mayor of Reed Station, a town five miles from Richville, parked his pick-up under the Tower and took deep breathing to another level to prevent his physical being from beginning to hack at the tall metal legs in hopes this "thing" could be brought down.

Phil was having marital difficulties with his wife Marge. Perhaps this tower represented a phallic symbol whereby he was feeling impotent.

Or perhaps it was only his city council members who berated him for his lack of foresight and lack of understanding as to what his constituents needed in the way of community services. This tower was an eyesore in his eyes. These thoughts of doing harm to this structure soon passed, and he put his genitals back between his legs and left.

If only Mayor Mervin LeRoy really knew the full impact of this tower, he may have spit out more speeches of self-proclaimed praise for his effort to make Richville the best small town on the map in the Midwest.

The future of the tower would play a role in just about every citizen of Richville's life—from the baptismal font to the last breath of the aged invalid in the Richville nursing home, sipping this precious liquid while seated in the wheelchair at the drinking fountain in the main hallway next to the nurses station (actually there was another fountain at the entrance to the home through the double doors on the left—down the hallway next to the main dining room—and the water always bordered on the frigid).

Let's not leave out the high school students when mentioning the tower. That is a story yet to be told.

And life goes on in Richville.

The Festival Committee Moves Ahead

With the late spring the blooms around town emerged; tulips were planted a few years ago in the park. They sprouted in early spring, in mid spring, and now in the middle of May.

The garden club with Missy Menage presiding as president helped plant thousands of these bulbs throughout Billings Gate Park; they even sought out elderly residents and helped plant these bulbs around their homes and gardens.

The Remembrance of Good Days Past committee moved ahead with the collective plans to bring this festival to fruition the weekend after Labor Day. A careful study around the region of other festivals showed only the Burrville Cabbage and Coleslaw Festival to be at the same time as the Good Old Days. Their mayor Heine Manoosh proclaimed his "bring it on attitude" to Mervin LeRoy at the county's semi-annual budget-and-spend-those-taxpayers'-dollars-but-not-in-a-wasteful-way meeting.

The ever feisty Heine threatened to dump a ton of sauerkraut in the middle of Billings Gate park and let the kraut flood the ever-weakening Richville sewer system, a threat he was never really serious about. Heine was the original small town (Burrville pop. 468) mayor and was prone to bluster a lot when threatened by these statistical challenges. The weekend after Labor Day stood as time for the Days of Remembrance festival. One item accomplished, several hundred more to face.

Richville, the town, came alive in late spring. Here in this most pleasant midwestern valley songbirds chirped their mating call while other animals such as squirrels, chipmunks, red foxes, badgers, and skunks made their way to the park in the neighborhoods.

The New Town Dump

A Site for Visitors to See Wildlife

And out of town the newly-developed town dump—a seeming safe haven for all of nature's wild species.

The occasional black bear would come to forage at this site. For the regions's citizens this site became a place to visit for a Kodak moment (many used their Brownie box camera to snap these critters). When these bears were spotted, the viewer would stand back, usually staying in their vehicles; these big creatures provided an adrenaline rush for these often squeamish, frightened viewers.

While some citizens complained that this area, though precisely marked and far enough outside of town not to really bother any of the neighborhood residents, would be a danger someday, most accepted the site as a place to actually dump trash, refuse, and the by-products of what Thorstan Veblan would call the "waste of the conspicuous consumption society."

Sightings at the dump became another plus and a commercial success for the Richville community. The mayor coined the expression "visit our Richville dump to see the animals forage. Join in the tailgating!"

Ever the promoter, the Mayor put an article in the region's newspaper The Times Herald promoting this dump as an "event worthy to visit." He wanted to sell shirts and open a restaurant near the site, refurbishing a small, old, vacated warehouse into a place that offers "the meat of nature's wild"—rabbit, squirrel, birds (pheasant in season), duck, and wild turkey. This idea would take time to implement—and was placed on another back burner.

And life goes on in Richville.

Tad "The Man" Reeves

Boy/Man Whirlwind Comes to Richville

The month of May in Richville rolled into June. Memorial weekend was the traditional time, after the last possible weather forecast of frost for late spring planting.

Residents and commercial growers alike put their seeds, seedlings, and vegetable plants into their well-mulched, well-composted, well-drained, and well-tilled soil.

This land in the valley was a fertile crescent for the region and, while many a sage agriculturist at an area agricultural school, these PhDs after much soil testing proclaimed this land and its soil only mediocre in fertility. The residents and especially the Gobbel brothers proved these academics wrong. The land provided opportunities to actually "make a startling, good living" as the brothers and others proved.

The school system was ready to ring out another year. There would be 118 seniors graduating from Richville High School. Dr. Wm DuVall PhD DDS went through the usual travails of problems a superintendent faces. He still wanted to move on to the newly-emerging intermediate district. He dealt with an elementary principal who, while chasing a child down a hallway (don't ask), tripped and broke her leg in three places and missed three months of school.

Also, the Richville board of education tried a new self-insured insurance program. That concept would have been okay had no one teacher had serious health issues; however, four staff members had serious heart issues, one a fatal attack while monitoring a hallway at the high school between classes.

The regional union was also beginning to make inroads in these rural communities, and Richville was no exception.

Dr. Wm DuVall claimed, to anyone who listened, bigger was not necessarily better. Teachers in Richville, while not highly compensated for their teaching efforts, relished being in a loving, caring community with many traditions already evidenced in the churches: the Chamber of Commerce; the annual Holiday Pride Parade the Friday after Thanksgiving) and the sing-along at the gazebo in Billings Gate Park and the sampling of the spiced liquids of the season: Swedish glug, holiday spiced rum, medieval mead, German beer, Irish spiced whiskey, and Russian vodka punch. An adult area was roped off to mark this place an adults only venue—no person under eighteen years of age allowed.

The Blooming Effervescent Richville Garden Club, LLC with Missy Menage at the helm also started the tradition of providing the flowers "for all occasions" at the many events in the community. The club started a rose garden in conjunction with the county's master gardening rose society. The garden now presides and flourishes at the back lot of Billings Gate park.

In the summer, the temperature warms over the land. The farm crops begin to gain stature, the corn more than knee high by the fourth of July, and the big green John Deere machines do their duty over the soil. This spoke volumes about the traditions and sanctity of this place called Richville, which, even though its people were busy and productive, they "always had time for you."

The school scene had its usual social news on who dated who; what sporting events were most important (the

Richville Blue Devil football team went 7-2 losing only to arch rivals Anchor Bay and non-league Burrville Muskrats); to what personalities made the most impact on the school scene (from dating to most influential student, etc.). The self-proclaimed assessor of the importance of these aforementioned superlatives was a bright, cheery, academically and socially advanced student Dana Jansen McElvy, daughter of Dean Beanie McElvy, Richville's prominent banker. Here is her story.

Dana

As the social gadabout at Richville High School, I have my pulse on everyone who is dating casually, permanently, committed to a significant other, or even, yuck, engaged to be married. I know all the romances, flings, jealousies, and misfortunes of the entire high school population. Quite a feat wouldn't you say?

At the beginning of this past school year a most persistent and enduring heart throb came to our school like a streak of lightning threatening to crack down the tallest sycamore tree in the neighborhood.

His name, Tad "The Man" Reeves as he was called. Tad was an ever-moving, ever-pulsing, bundle of perpetual motion, always ready to plant a few words of endearment into our tuned-in teen minds.

Tad could turn on all the hearts of the young ladies in the high school or could crush the egos with equal skill. He had a southern charm and flair, the likes of which had not ever been seen in our small Midwest community.

To most of the girls in the high school, Tad seemed like a Huck Finn—a character with a laid-back demeanor, slightly mischievous, with a constant grin on his oval face as wide as the old chuck hole on Monroe Street.

Once in our midst, and after "getting used to y'all," he exploded on the school's social scene. Tad was everywhere at once like a mini social revolution. His mind and body whirled in constant motion.

At precisely 2:08 PM, four minutes before the end of a long week during the first month of the school year, a loud bang exploded in the far end of the senior hallway. We seniors who were in the same chemistry class as Tad knew he had smuggled white phosphorus out of the lab and placed it in a warm locker.

Several of us were dispatched to Mr. Rumlou's office where we read the riot act. The police would be summoned. All lockers would be checked for "illegal substances," and Randy the drug-sniffing K-9 German shepherd would be called in to sniff out the perpetrator.

My immediate circle of friends thought this stunt to be dangerous and foolish. Why did Tad have to test the authority and seemingly violate our precious health and safety? Only Tad seemed to know.

Even though the higher authorities in the school were putting pressure on us to turn in the guilty party, we remained mum and no one ratted on Tad.

Tad was a potent mix of young almost out of control youth and half-grown man who had us all under his spell. We seemed to be cast in his spell, waiting for the next prank to be enacted.

A week after the white phosphorus incident, a high-powered electrical storm ambushed Richville with accompanying high winds and grape-sized hail.

I had just finished my sixth hour aerobics class and was in the shower when a power surge bolted through the locker room and the lights flickered, dimmed, and went out.

Twenty-five students were in a state of frenzy as we were in various stages of dressing. My hair was soaked and clung to my back as we blindly tried to locate towels and find the right clothes to put on. It seemed strange that only the girls locker room had lost its lights. An announcement told us a back-up generator was about to be activated and not to panic.

The following morning before school Tad bumped into me in the food commons. "Hey, Dana, how did you like being in the dark yesterday? Did the boogyman get ya?"

I flashed an anguished stare into Tad's deep blue eyes. I then noticed his mouth was open and turned upward in a pumpkin-like grin. Suddenly, I burst out laughing. "So it was you who left us in the dark, you old hunk of mischief."

Tad was, after all, in an electrical wiring class at the area vocational trade academy. This latest feat, I suppose, was just another step as part of his apprenticeship training I said mockingly to myself.

"Wait till you see what I have planned today during lunch" Tad burst out.

I couldn't wait. The first three hours plodded by. My calc class was like a dirge; my bio-chem class crept painfully along; even my econ class seemed like a bad nightmare. Break for lunch came none too soon. Tad and I had the same break.

As I entered the commons, there was Tad, clipboard in hand, taking signatures.

"Dana, Dana, sign my food protest petition will ya?

"We're goin' to change the quality of food in this place, make it better, more wholesome, with more variety," Tad proclaimed to me and anyone within earshot of his voice.

He went on to explain: "Since we have a closed campus, we demand better quality vittles in this joint. Did you know this whole food program is just a money-making operation? They buy pizza from Hungry Sam and double the price to us poor victims; plus we only get one type of pizza—with those gaseous pepperonis. That's enough to tear your ever-lovin' guts out."

Without blinking twice, I signed. Again, Tad's charm combined with reckless boldness overcame any thought of hesitation. My name on this petition might mean a reprimand from the administration. Think, Dana, think.

Suddenly, Mr. Towers the principal entered the commons. "What gives here? Tad, what are you up to—no good, I suspect?"

Tad made his case to Mr. Towers on his territory, in his office. The meeting lasted over an hour.

What was discussed remained a secret between the two adversaries. Tad, again in his usual casual manner, confronted an issue that students in the high school grumbled about for years, but said nothing and did nothing to address.

Tad was not suspended for raising these concerns. In fact, the school board formed a committee to bring a wider variety of menu items for lunches, even working with the local vegetable growers (i.e. Gobbel Bros.) to invest in the health of Richville's youth.

Even a school breakfast program was discussed, which may start the beginning of the next school year.

Could it have been Tad's protest that single-handedly moved the school board off dead center and into a new vision for the hungry hoard of students in the Richville school system?

Small communities often spawn eccentric, but well-meaning characters who are often considered aloof, anti-social, or sometimes just plain scary.

One such character was Barny Bard, a lifetime Richville resident, trader in antiques, junk, pleasures, pure and decadent (this saying on his business card) who opened up his acreage one fall to those youth of driving age and spectators to participate in the first (maybe) annual mud bog competition.

He proclaimed, "Bring your vehicles and farm tractors to my marsh at high noon this October Sunday." Word spread quickly around town among the youth.

Tad "The Man" Reeves would revel in this event. He had customized a '32 Ford coup with an engine that roared super horsepower and the absence of any muffler. His tires were race-ready and twice the size of regular tires; thus, the body of the car was lifted to accommodate these large wheels.

Other high school youth brought out their own version of race-worthy vehicles; there was a modified Chevy coup, a World War II Jeep (worthy of a mud bog terrain), the Carlotto's '47 Studebaker Stake Truck (modified); and assorted John Deere tractors.

Even Petey Snodgrass Sr. brought his motorcycle made up of scrap parts from the local scrap yard.

Barny flooded a football field sized area and ground his marsh so that regular loam and fertile soil turned to a mushy, sludgy, muddy tract of land.

Not to be outdone, Tad was in the first event, raring to show his fellow buddies his coup named "The Croc" would successfully negotiate this muck and mush and would win the overall event.

Barny put up a Tin Cup as first prize and would allow the first, second, and third place winners to choose an antique from his store (fifty dollar value or under).

Barny would set the rules; his decision as to first, second, and third place would be final. If the event was successful—meaning everyone was on their best behavior and there was no alcohol or smoking that strange-smelling hemp called a reefer—this could turn into a tradition.

While most vehicles stalled and became stuck in this muck, Tad persevered and made it through to the next round.

Tad's demeanor was light and cheery and each successive victory only brought out a bigger smile to his face. His six-foot-plus, muscled frame and easy-going manner again drove the many girls in attendance into a tizzy. Only Molly McDernid, the lone female, entered the race with her family's Woody; this move she would regret for a long time.

The last heat pitted Dickey McQuirter in his World War II, standard-operational Jeep and Tad in his modified '32 Ford coup.

Tad raced across the field spitting sludge and muck everywhere throwing up a rooster tail behind him. The Jeep kept pace.

Barny Bard was standing at the finish line. Dickey and Tad both raced across the finish line at almost the same time.

Barny raised his right arm and pointed to Tad as the winner—a photo-like finish.

Tad emerged from the vehicle and fell on his back in the mud doing a mud angel. Other students, onlookers, and participants followed suit and over a hundred people that day in Barny Bard's marsh began flapping their wings in the mud like angels sputtering away to the heavens.

I, Dana Jansen McElvy, didn't join in this mud bath party, but I felt the inner glow and warmth the scene created. This scene, this day, would be etched in my memory and would return whenever I needed it to regress and find comfort from my days in this rural, midwestern town of Richville.

Tad again had provided the spark; we acted like small children growing in stature, but not sure of our boundaries yet.

Tad "The Man" Reeves expanded our small-town, limited boundaries and told us by his example it was all right to have good, clean fun. The time for serious pursuits would come soon enough.

A few weeks later on a Monday morning found the usual social clatter around our lockers. I noticed Tad saunter to his locker with his usual lively gait. He was, as usual, surrounded by his buddies, several of whom had partied the previous weekend at Bard's barn. I had heard of this barn blast and politely turned down an invitation to attend.

Pam Nolle, my class friend, suddenly gasped. "Look at Tad's skull—completely bare, no hair, skinhead, bald as an egg."

I commented that maybe this was a new trend, a pace-setting moment in time. Tad had apparently launched a new rocket in his arsenal of social behavior.

Throughout the day, eyes were glued to Tad's bald dome. His whole face seemed bigger, his grin wider, and his eyes seemed to sparkle even brighter than when he courted a full head of hair. Tad remained the center of attention and again reveled in the moment.

Over the next week, Tad converted a few of his buddies to his clean-shaven club, but it was not a widespread movement around the high school.

Right before Thanksgiving break, Tad approached me with something he wanted to "confide." We met in the food commons right when school was out for the day. "Dana, I've always liked you and I value you as a confident—I'd appreciate you listening to me very closely now."

I fumbled my thoughts and didn't know now what he meant, what was so important. His face crinkled and his frown lines became pronounced.

"What are you talking about, what do you want? How can I help you?" I blurted out in short, breathy phrases.

"Regardless, Dana, no matter what happens to me, I'm going to be climbing the Richville Water Tower during senior spirit week next May. I'm doin' it for our class, my last prank and one for tradition.

"What's going to happen to you? Are you going to disappear like some infamous magic act? Now you see me now you don't?" I laughed nervously at his now serious nature.

Tad continued, "Be calm for a moment, Dana. I'm going back to Florida for a while to see my mom. I'll be back after Christmas break. I haven't told anyone else yet. I can't tell you why just now. Just remember the good times we've enjoyed together. Don't forget me, young lady—carry my memory for our sake. I'm beginnin' to have deep feelings for you, but I know it wouldn't be right, right now—you and me a couple. You're smart, Dana; you see through me. I hope you see the real me, the other Tad."

My heart pounded, my eyes were watery. Why was I tearing up? I didn't want this moment to happen this way. Why couldn't I just laugh and wonder what Tad's next prank would be? I just wanted him to push the limit, have some fun, and put us all on. Now he had to get serious. And he's leaving for awhile. Why? What's happening?

Tad was gone in a blur. He turned to go and I thought I saw him blink and smile. I followed his shaven head out the side door of the commons into the chilly late fall afternoon.

The Christmas season in my family and in our town of Richville came and went as a blur. Family and friends gathered at our home for the traditional festivities. Our tree, usually the most ornate in the neighborhood, glistened with baubles and sparkles.

Our family's traditions went back over twenty five years. My mother, true to her Italian heritage, cooked pizza, fritta, pizzalas, calzones, and made a true Italian treat—spungone.

We drank my father's homemade red wine and grappa and munched on Italian cookies and homemade fudge—my specialty.

I thought of Tad and what he was missing here—the joy of family and friends, and even some of those odd characters in Richville who might stop by and toast us "to have good cheer and a spirited holiday season."

We weren't back in school for even a week when the town became blanketed in the first real storm of the season. I received a letter from Tad.

"I won't be back for a few more weeks. I would like you to come to our house my first day back January 18th at 4:00 PM." The letter was brief and to the point.

Why such a definite time and date, I wondered? The day arrived. I would finally see where Tad lived and become privy to "The Man" behind the scenes.

He lived a mile outside of town along M19 down a rural dirt corrugated road in an area of ram-shackled huts like bungalows and vast vacant acreages dotted with no trespassing and no hunting signs.

Four o'clock sharp. I peered over the picket fence, which was now piled high with several inches of new snow.

His property was completely fenced off with the exception of the west side in which a wall of stones and boulders stood. Several generations ago the Carlucci family sold these former inhabitants these rocks, but the job was never completed.

I looked up to see the old Italianate farmhouse, which, to me, was neither friend nor foe, mostly just a drab, very tired looking structure.

Old laced curtains adorned the front bay windows. I sidestepped an old rusted Schwinn bike and several metal objects, which may have been car parts, on my way to the front steps.

I rang the bell; it didn't buzz only clicked and no response came from inside. I did hear a chime from a grandfather clock on the other side of the front door.

I banged on the front door. The screen rattled. Inside Tad's Aunt Bess peered at me from within.

She opened the door. "You must be Dana. Tad's expecting you. Follow me."

She led me to his bedroom, a large room toward the back of the house converted from what looked like an old-fashioned, screened-in porch.

My heart leapt into my throat as I entered Tad's room. He was laying on top of the bed with what looked like a turban on his head. He was dressed in fatigues with large wool socks bundling his feet.

"Hi ya, kid—where ya been all my life?" He suddenly became very animated.

I wanted to scream, to ask a million questions, but I only wrinkled the creases in my worry lines on my face and frowned.

Again Tad continued, "Let me tell ya where I've been—what happened—why I'm back.

"For over a year I've had horrible headaches on and off at the base of my neck. I slept long hours at times hoping they would go away. I took aspirin; nothing helped. Finally I went to my doctor. After an intensive cat scan, a tumor the size of a golf ball was found growing at the base of my neck. My chance for survival was so so, about ten percent. It was discovered at the beginning of our school year.

"I wanted this senior year to be the most enjoyable, the most thrilling, the most fun-filled of any high school class at Richville ever. Did I succeed, Dana?"

Before I could respond, Tad continued. "I had to go back to Florida to have the operation; now I'm back with Aunt Bess.

"I've gone through what is called adjuvant chemotherapy. I've taken some intramuscular anti-cancer drugs and had some side effects, especially at first. My hair has fallen out. I've lost my appetite and dropped over thirty pounds. My toes and fingers are continually burning and my feet and lower legs are swelled to twice their size. I drink a gallon and a half of water a day and am always going to the bathroom," he said, continuing to explain his condition.

"Other than that I feel like I could still pull some good pranks with the best of them. Oh, I've lost part of my hearing in my left ear, but that's not so bad. Another thing—Mrs. Blackman comes over to give me my lessons so I will definitely graduate on time.

He further explained, "I'm going to be kind of a guinea pig with this whole tumor cancer thing. I've always wanted to be ahead of my time—so here's my chance."

I couldn't contain myself any longer and practically screamed out, "What's going on? What are the chances now of living? Of getting better?"

Tad sprung up on his elbows and burst out with a warm smile. "Kid I'll be on that water tower Saturday May 8th with our other classmates; take that to the bank."

As early spring called the robins back to our state, and the forsythia and lilacs began emitting their flowers, the atmosphere at school turned to spring break and Richville new beginnings.

Our art class was accompanied to Paris, France by Petey Snodgrass Sr., town cultural scholar. I declined the offer.

I went to see Tad a few times. Sometimes he was pale and his skin was very dry. Other times he was cherry with a punk-ish complexion and he was talkative. He was, at times, slurping some sort of bullion soup and seemed to have gained back a few pounds.

The morning of May 8th was warm, sunny, and the birds were chirping. The sun started to reflect off the gigantic water tower like a spotlight shining off a bald head.

That evening would find a select few from the senior class climbing the side of the tower, horizontal beam to horizontal beam, to a ladder for the final ascent to the top.

Sundown came quickly, then nightfall. The team arrived, all seniors. There was Matt Flarety, Jim Thomas, Stacey McDonald (the only female), and Scott Menage (son of Missy Menage—Garden Club president). I came to observe, but no Tad "The Man" Reeves.

The ascent began. Carefully the group climbed from beam to beam. Halfway up, a platform protruded from the tower. The group rested. Still no Tad Reeves.

Again the climb commenced. Only a few more feet and the ladder would be reached.

The group began climbing the ladder. Only twenty more feet to reach the top of the tower. Matt would place the Richville sing on the tower with all the seniors having signed it and the Blue Devil symbol boldly printed in the middle.

Suddenly a figure at the bottom of the tower shouted up to the climbers nearing the top. "I'm here, y'all!" Tad proclaimed with joy in his voice.

"I'll be with ya before the alligators in the bayou know it's feedin' time.

"Hi ya, Dana, 'The Man' is here to put our class on the map," Tad said as he began the climb.

Tad seemed to leap upward; he climbed hand over hand on the beams. He seemed to reach the ladder in record time.

When he reached the top he was out of breath, wheezing uncontrollably, and sweating profusely, but with that ever-present mischievous grin on his face.

Tad took over the proceedings. "We're all here together, the Richville senior class tower crew. We're ready to howl, ready to rumble, ready to plant our souls on this H_2O monument for posterity's sake.

Even though I was at the bottom, I felt our mission was accomplished—a feeling of being one with everyone there on that Tower, a feeling of being one with our fellow seniors, our school, and our community.

That pitch black night the moon shone more brightly; the chill of the evening was thrilling.

I'm sure my goose bumps were from being thrilled by the moment, not from the coolness of that late spring evening.

I was mixed with feelings for Tad, his present condition, and how much time we would have together.

We ended the evening at Cooky's Café. Although Tad's demeanor was upbeat and vibrant, his face was withered and drawn.

Other seniors were at the café, and Tad bantered with his peers. "Hey, Eric, no water tower in the world can hold me down. Steve, old boy, I'd like to see you climb to the top of your pole barn let alone the top of the Richville Water Tower. Pete [senior class president] we put our emblem higher than any other class, put something about this great event in that time capsule you're planning.

"Tonight while up there with the stars I mooned the moon," Tad repeated and everyone screamed with laughter.

Tad turned to me: "Take me to my palace, Dana."

At his door, we parted ways and said our goodbyes. Why did I suddenly feel such finality to this moment? With our time over the school year together, this evening, and the Tad "The Man" pranks echoing with fond remembrance in my mind.

Tad reached over and gently pulled me near to him and kissed me. It was spontaneous and generous. The glow inside me was further kindled.

I floated on the sidewalk only glancing back once. Tad was gone. My face flushed and tears flowed—a moment to record two people's love for each other; a statement but not a commitment; deep affection, but no everlasting ring.

Two days later Tad pass away in his sleep. The tumor had spread and reached the point where it had terminated all his brain functions . . . no comatose state, no feeblemindedness, no remission this time, no long goodbyes.

Tad knew what the headaches meant—he planned the school year carefully—but the spontaneity was his alone and the way he positively affected all of us was a testament to his southern charm and endearing mischievous personality.

With Tad, there was no self pity, no maniacal moments, no gloating of his achievements. And now gone. We would remember Tad as that whirlwind boy-man from the Gator state who came to us in Richville with a charm that lit all our fires while his was so abruptly silenced.

The End

Memories, not dulled with time, but sharp with reflection is what we have left and, after all, isn't that the most poignant kind? The kind that lasts not just for a school year, but through all of time, rain or shine?

Tad's Aunt Bess planned the funeral with the Reverend Harold Huether presiding. The Richville Greater Lutheran United Church was filled with students and members of the community.

Often what happens in a school does not get out into public view. Tad "The Man" Reeves was the exception.

As Reverend Huether proclaimed, Tad helped anyone at anytime for almost any reason with his acts of kindness and generosity.

"We should remember this kind spirit and young man of virtue," the reverend went on to say.

Students and citizens alike stood to proclaim their fond remembrances of Tad. The Gobbel brothers remembered when their big John Deere harvester broke down. Tad was there to repair the gigantic machine.

Petey Snodgrass, the self-proclaimed town scholar, told the audience "We should remember Tad in our upcoming first annual Days of Remembrance festivities."

The church choir dedicated the hymn "Peace in the Valley" to Tad's life; the choir director Lou Frazzini wanted the song to be the official hymn of Richville. It seemed appropriate now that this hymn would mark a tradition as the "hymn of the Richville community." Let other church denominations put up their own hymn in debate or forever hold their tongues in peace.

"I am tired and weary but I must toil on till the Lord comes to call me away; where the morning is bright and the Lamb is the light and the night is as fair as the day. There the flow'rs will be blooming, the grass will be green, and the skies will be clear and serene. The sun ever shines giving one endless beam and no clouds there will ever be seen.

There'll be Peace in the Valley for me someday. There'll be Peace in the Valley for me. I pray no more sorrow and sadness or trouble will be. There'll be Peace in the Valley for me. Amen.

Tad's Aunt Bess had a headstone for Tad in Richville Cemetery of Eternal Rest and Enshrinement. On his headstone read Tad Reeves—a young man of gracious honesty and pure heart R.I.P.

Some of the high school students, especially the seniors, echoed these same sentiments on the Richville Loving Stone in Billings Gate Park.

The Richville school system would soon be dismissed for the long stretch of summer. Some of the community expressed strong opinions that the system should go year around. The school board tabled these arguments again and again so youth just like the late blossoming trees burst forth with an energy to spark a revolution all over town or, as with the rotting chestnut trees, cause irreparable harm to the town's sewer system. This proposition seemed like a toss-up.

And life goes on in Richville.

Rich Ribald

Raw Rhetoric from the Halls of Richville High School

The story of Tad "The Man" Reeves is a never-ending, heartfelt drama that played out in this small tightly-knit community.

There are other stories of youth in this town, however, which seem futile, wayward, out of control, and idiosyncratic if not downright disturbing.

Take the young man Bob Hartly known around the community as Bike Bob, a young man now in his thirties riding endlessly on the same trails every day rain or shine, whose diminished mental state is evident as he wheels his Schwinn Special down the heavily tree-lined streets of Richville, shouting out at the onlookers, vacant lots, or to nobody in particular—"Look at me—no-hands Bob—bet you can't ride like me." With his Cheshire grin, although vacant and innocent enough on the inside, there was evidence of a lack of interpersonal skills. Some said he was dim-witted, others said he was a menace to the neighborhoods through which he traveled.

The local police watched him intently, but publicly said there was nothing they could do to take him off the streets and put his riding ways permanently to rest.

He lived with an uncle just on the outskirts of town in a ramshackled old farmhouse and many stray felines, hens, roosters, and a few sheep, which roamed the property. Some onlookers who drove by this mess said these animals had free reign to the main dwelling and wandered in an out of the facility.

Often characters of high school age lived on the fringe of respectability, drifting in and out of the school scene, some staying in school yet going to extremes to "be their own person"; some gothic-like characters; some tough (on the surface); some in and out of the county's juvenile detention facility.

A favorite game that recently emerged at the high school was a real-life version of the Dungeons and Dragons game using the city's sewer system and various points of interest around the community as landmarks—the great water tower, the town dump, the vacant (haunted?) mansion just outside of town, the Eternal Rest Cemetery. Also at the outskirts of town were marked spots for the game.

The town fathers with the local police put an end to the Dungeons and Dragons game.

Then there was Dean "Bad Boy" Bergen, now serving seven to ten at the state pen for armed robbery who, a year ago before the many hold ups, ruptured the big gas line pump whose gas filled the school system's buses. The gasoline leaked underground into the adjacent football field, causing the team to have to play their home games at the Burrville football field. Both communities, which were rivals on many fronts, coalesced to request this Dean boy be punished to the maximum extent of the law. He was and spent six months in the county jail. But now back in the community, he was more enraged than ever, thus the armed robberies. Captured after holding up one of the Rapid Rory's convenience stores—off to the state pen for this once cherubic youth who grew up in Richville with, one thought, decent parents, loving siblings, and a once ninety-miles-per-hour fast ball in little league on the first place regional team, the Fighting Hornets. Now his life is in ruins . . . choices, choices.

Now we come to a youth one Rob Criten. His slide into depression was gradual. His home environment chaotic and unpredictable. His story, as it adds to the fabric of life in this small town with its many malleable layers of living breathing existence, is worth telling. Rich, ribald, raw rhetoric from the halls of Richville High School, here is *The Broken Mirror—A Slide Into Depression*, one adolescent's auto biographical account of that fateful fall into no man's land.

Rob

Enter my domain at your own risk. My teen mind is currently reeling with angst and a feeling of foreboding, gloom, and unbridled anxiety, which is about to be unleashed into a non-caring world of utter disgust and futility.

Oh yes, my name Rob Criten. My perch from which I spew these invectives is none other than Richville High School, a typical eclectic brew of teens journeying through an electrostatic inferno called education—metaphorically being engulfed within a python-like creature never to go back to the mouth or light of day and eventually to be thrust out that posterior end to have to fend in a world of strange creatures, bizarre underworld beings, and ultimately being told by a parent "No, I'm not paying for even part of your car insurance anymore—you're on your own, bud."

As my senior year passes at Richville, I try to put myself in a self-induced trance-like state to dull my perception of reality in order to function day to day.

I do listen intently to my instructors who, in their own disciplines, tell me about life's inevitable pathways and the life aging processes I will have to inevitably endure.

My health teacher Mr. Bryan calls it a homeo static balancing act. He says stay within the rules, possibly occasionally straying, but having the wherewithal to pull oneself back in line, having a quick reflexive jerk around the neck to reawaken that sense of having to put one's house in order. Get back to some semblance of reality to see, at least, the cause and effect of one's behavior.

In my psych class, Mr. Whitman breaks apart the mind into the id, ego, and superego. "Keep these parts in balance," he preaches "and life for the average Joe becomes tolerable."

Even in my drama class, Ms. Schlater says we beings are either antagonists or protagonists, a life force with a beginning, middle, and end. Our audience, she further states, will know when that echoic climax occurs—when the summation of all parts of the play burst forth; when the audience wide-eyed knows why the story line evolved to this point; that the subsequent conclusions show that most conflicts are resolved. The audience would stand and cheer and applaud. They would walk out of the darkened theatre with a new sense of rebirth, a new sense of reality, and a chance once again to start life anew—no lasting bruises, no ugly scars, no permanent deformities to hinder one's day-to-day grind through life's labyrinth.

I have attempted to apply these maxims and principles to my eighteen-year-old, one-hundred-eighty-pound slightly paunchy male frame.

Staying homeostatically balanced in such a fast paced techno-studded, educational, theatrical environment requires steady nerves, far-reaching internal resources, both technical and human, an engaging dispositions—except in Ms. McGrunders's fourth-hour geometry II class where we are required to memorize proofs ad nauseam and we have break B as our lunch break and have to come back to class for another twenty minutes of mental torture. Once I leave a class I always figured I was done for the hour.

My formal schooling here at Richville over the years has been sporadic at best. There haven't been many subjects or teachers I've felt from whom I learned much. I always thought we should just give our teachers a list of ideas we wanted to pursue and then go learn on our own. I know, I know thirty or more teens actually using their brains all at once in a class would blow the minds of most teachers. My thoughts turn to finding alternative sources of fuel for small engines, especially on my snow mobile, or how to work toward becoming more racially-tolerant of each other. The energy we could generate from these true-life learning experiences would really blow the roof off old Richville High and would shower mega-watt light through our halls of gloom and doom.

"Rob! Rob! Daydreaming again I see!" Ms. McGrunder's cat-like presence is ready to strike like some general thirsting for the first blood of battle.

"Rob, we have just two minutes 'til break; for the last time, respect the Pythagorean Theorem verbatim."

"Sorry ma'am," I answer timidly. "I'm just thinking about my job after school and how to cut corners."

Oh yes, back to you my public. Before I continue my sordid tale, let me preface any remarks by saying my past has indeed been checkered. To continue, I've been in five school systems up to the eighth grade, all public.

My parents split after my eighth-grade year, and I was home-schooled for a year. My mother signed on with the American Eagle School of Perpetual Learning. I sat at the kitchen table and my mother fed me great ideas from Western and Eastern civilizations, basic math concepts, and I wrote every day in a diary. This was bare-boned learning at best, but I missed my friends in the public school and being able to do impressions of the Beatles for them. My Paul McCartney is especially moving. I do a Mick Jagger, but I don't have the facial expression quite down yet.

I'm sorry about my parents splitting up, but my dad is a full-fledged alcoholic and pot user. He would go on binges and not be home for weeks at a time. My mom would keep taking him back. They'd break up, make up, break up, and make up again and again.

In his better moments, Dad was a major league turdball always claiming to have conquered Mt. Everest or some such metaphorical mountain. In his worst moments, he was a demonic wife-beating, son-slapping SOB capable of mass destruction on a major league level. One of his claims was to have lived with Charley Manson just weeks before those tragic killings and getting out of Charley's clutches just in time. He claims to have signed papers that made him part of the Manson family. I could neither prove nor disprove this bit of our family's sordid past.

Now he and his father live in their own flat in Garland Heights about ten miles outside of Richville.

My mom now is seeing, dating, going with, otherwise living with another man. He helps her with the house payments and other living expenses.

I liked him even though he was a big, imposing dude who never seemed to shave or shower. He was always making grunting noises.

These noises were in reaction to my mother's wishes or commands as her moods and the occasion called for it.

Go to the store and get me some lettuce, Honey. "Ugh or uh" would be his curt reply. We didn't really bond well as ole Henry had a habit of staying a few weeks then cutting out on us. We weren't really a family, but mom pretended we were. I suppose she leads a semi-rich fantasy life.

I don't exactly have a male or female role model to follow so I follow those entertainers who are popular. As I said, I imitate these individuals—Mick Jagger and most of the Beatles namely Paul McCartney. I was almost fired last week at Sigmans Fine Dining, a restaurant in Richville, for imitating the Mick while bussing tables.

Good ole boy Tim Sigman the day manager confronted me and screamed (my perception) "One more outburst like that, young man, and you're through workin' for me."

I blushed, bowed my head, swallowed my pride, and went on bussing my tables in silence. I usually bounce back from these snippy moments of frustration, but lately they've been building to a crescendo of biting hatred and anger. Who do these adults think they are?

Is there no one who would help our cause? We free thinkers need outlets. We are performers, but without a stage, the performance is dull and the lights go out.

Lately, I have been given to fits of nagging hopelessness bordering on despair. This blackness surrounding me engulfs my persona.

My gift for gab, making my peers laugh, and occasionally making adults chuckle is being snuffed out. Play the dull roll of a stiff, somber, stupored, soul-less being, a lackey whose only play left is to be a senseless turdball without feelings, without a sense of purpose. Is there no one around me who understands my plight? I am a being caught in the jaws of eternal damnation; down, down, down I go spiraling into an empty abyss.

I've skipped a few days of school this semester; nothing really interests me there anymore. Mom has taken up with another slimeball, a real dirt bag. I've argued with him several times about his health habits; he drinks incessantly, eats any time of the day or night, leaves garbage lying around, prances around in his BVDs, and generally stinks to high heaven.

I think his real name is Max Reisner. He has several AKAs and is wanted for bad check passing in several states. He used to run stolen cars from Tennessee up north, changing the VIN numbers and selling them to a broker who auctioned them off. Now, he just lies around wallowing in his own filth in my presence day in and day out.

My mother, with her usual good taste, found this sleezebag at Bar 31, so named because of the mile road it perches on. They became drinking buddies. She brought this geezer home to have the run of our palatial digs—really a three-room apartment overlooking Richville's finest DPW garbage dump where every night, if the wind blows right (or wrong), our olfactory lobes are filled with the remains of the finest cuisine consumed by Richville's residents from Italian, to Greek, to Chinese, to just plain down home cookin'. We don't have to go out on route 15 to sample the road kill; it comes to us packaged as refuse unlimited, Inc. straight from the kitchen of Richville's rich and infamous, fine dining at its best.

I couldn't be more down in my own festering dumps. I quit my job at Sigman's last week. I rarely attend school anymore, and my days are drifting from meaningless nights into meaningless tomorrows. When one loses a sense of hope, self-pity takes over. There is no more edginess to my attitude as I have no attitude. My friends have all but deserted me. Even they don't want to wallow in my self-inflicted despair. My reasons for getting up in the morning just faded away. I sought to be a light to the world, a beacon of truth, a torch bearer showing people the true path to self-fulfillment . I just can't stand the self-torture, the absolute pitch black numbness; the abandonment of self. I'm not running from anything anymore and I'm not running to anything. What goals I used to have, have been dashed beyond repair. I can't give others hope if I'm trapped in my own cloak of hopelessness. I used to be good at selling my wares, my persona, my smile, but now I'm a frigid, not even cryogenically, frozen excuse for a homosapien.

I sit in my darkened room, shade drawn, bed unmade, clothes strewn everywhere, the James Dean picture peeling off the wall, old Metallica posters crumpled in a corner, and Rolling Stones concert posters ripped and shredded lying limply on my dresser.

My collections of matchbox cars are also scattered about my room along with my comic book collection.

My old trombone rots in my closet; I used to play in the seventh and eighth grades but gave it up because of the Nazi-like band director who made us goose step up and down, up and down the football field. I always booted the person in front of me in his coccyx.

At least over the last month I lost my paunch since food is but a wasteful bit of extravagance. I'm down to one hundred forty pounds and wilting away. My eyes have become accustomed to the darkened room; it's the light that now blinds me.

One of mom's more insignificant beaus, Ole Max only stayed a few weeks. He left to run some more hot cars from the denizens of southern auto graveyards to the more lucrative motor yards of the north.

Now Mom can go out again and prowl the area bars and bring home another fine gentleman with low brow tastes and a sub-human mind-set.

But again I'm wallowing in my own loathing and self-despair. I try sleeping in my most misfit of states, the seeming end to my world coming closer to reality.

It is 3:00 AM when the phone rings. My mom is out after hours prowling the bars or having picked up another scumnut.

The voice on the other end asked me if I was Rob Criten, the son of Andrew Criten.

"Yes," came my terse reply.

"Then come to the Banger County Morgue immediately," the voice on the other end commanded. "There's been a fire at your father's home. We need a family member to identify his body. There is also another gentleman perhaps you can identify."

Now when I want to feel nothing, to have every pore of my being void of feeling, I instead feel a mad rush of blood and emotions coursing through these once-empty pores.

I drop to my knees, weak with exhaustion. Tears drip streams of moisture on my cheeks.

My father, the most absent of beings in my life, now occupies all my thoughts. I feel attached to him more than ever. I thought he was out of my life forever.

The other body in question may be Grandpa. He, too, is not really a part of my life anymore either.

I dress, find my wallet and car keys, and, in a daze, drive to the county hospital. My hands are clammy, my breathing labored, my head aching with grief; I feel a sense of loss, confusion, despair and thought why me, Lord, why me?

Upon arriving at the old white marbled gothic structure, I race to the information desk. I identify myself to the receptionist and ask where the morgue was located. She looks at me with a bored animated detached look and calls security.

"Ralph here will escort you to the back of the hospital to the morgue, young man."

The guard, not saying a word, motions with his hand to follow him.

I am left at a door heavily plated with steel. The smell is antiseptic, but with other odors not familiar to me.

I knock—nothing. I knock again and an older, white-haired, craggy, pock-marked-faced man opens the door. He doesn't look at me; his face seems to count the marbled tiles on the floor.

I know I was interrupting him performing some great work of art—in this case doing an autopsy on some poor departed soul.

"I'm Rob Criten here to identify two bodies, possibly my father and grandfather."

Without raising his head, the pathologist beckons me to two slabs of marble another white-lab-smocked worker pulls out from the wall.

He removes the shroud. I peer at the exposed, blackish-graying masses of burnt flesh. The sour charcoal smelling stench makes my eyes water.

I view their heads and saw hollowed eye sockets. Their faces once giving of life now blackened from the fire that raged through their home, a place I visited on occasion—a place I came to feel was my second home, now, too, burnt to the ground.

I sob uncontrollably. The bright halogen lights of the morgue blind me. A feeling of extreme frigidity comes over me. Goose bumps appear on my arms and face. I suddenly hurl my TV dinner on the slab my father is prostrated on; mucus from my nostrils drips onto the cold marble floor.

The air is suddenly punctuated with sound. "Do you recognize these two bodies, young man?" the pathologist questions me matter-of-factly.

"He's my old man, my father—my flesh in blood. The other body is my grandfather, Gramps."

The older doctor again states matter-of-factly, "They must have had quite a party what with their pot and alcohol all over their premises. Too bad their space heater was kicked over, causing the fire . . . awful way to go," his voice trailing to a low murmur.

The other technician has me sign some papers, asks me about my next of kin, and states the authorities will interview me in the near future. Do I have a plan to dispose of the bodies? He addresses me in a formal matter-of-fact way.

The drive home is slow and deliberate. I call Mom from the hospital and still no answer. I have no other relative to turn to.

I go home and stay in my room for two days, refusing to answer the phone. The truant officer from the district calls and will be paying me a visit this week. Two of my co-workers from Sigman's Restaurant call and wonder why I quit—let's get together for a chat is their message. Another male punk suitor calls for my mother and wants to take her to the big stock car race in Ubley that weekend. That poor slob doesn't know what trouble he's getting into.

I confine myself in my room. I wonder who and when from the law enforcement agency will be contacting me. Also, what arrangements will be made for my dad and Gramps? I don't know if anyone else from the family will step forward to make these arrangements. And where is my mom? What does she know, if anything?

My mind is numb trying to picture my old man falling asleep as his brain becomes jelly—like on one of his acid or pot party trips. Usually he is just a party of one—a self-absorbed, tortured soul who abandoned us for the immediate gratification of sucking on a weed stick or going into cyber space on an acid trip. How ironic he would burn down his own house; I consider his self-induced fire just to be the shortcut to Hell he always deserved. And poor Gramps just went along for the horrible ride. Goodbye, Gramps.

I am always amazed at myself for not going along with Dad's drinking and pot-smoking when he first offered me a weed and a brew—at the same time no less.

I look at the mirror hanging on my closet door. My face is withered, bulging bags under my eyes, a sadness on the contours of my brows, my lips pursed tightly. For once what I am feeling inside matches the outer demeanor of skin on my skull.

Wallowing in a barnyard full of self-pity, I think my days on earth might be numbered. Where is the button for forgiving oneself, for showing compassion to others, for seeing life in a clearer light where guilt, self-hatred, and self-pity are swept away?

This story can end now if I only have the guts to make that slipknot, trigger that 35mm. Where's the cyanide when you really need it?

And to think all my role models, family members who could give me some advice, are either walled up in some maximum security prison, out on some bottle binge of their own, or, like me, holed up in some flat, squeezing liquor out of their food stamps, declaring themselves psychologically, emotionally, and financially bankrupt.

I once read where an individual can write his own life script one scene at a time and can visually work his way through any dilemma one small step at a time. As an avid movie fan I can begin to see myself larger than life, up there on that big blank surface, showing the audience how much resolve I really have, how I will not be tied to the tracks by any Snidely Whiplash or made to give in to a brow beating bombastic Sydney Greenstreet in a scene from *The Maltese Falcon*.

The phone rings interrupting my train-off-its-tracks thinking. I answer, not knowing who or what agencies want my attention.

"This is your mother—surprise, surprise! I went to visit your Aunt Sophie downstate. Remember her? Your favorite aunt? I'll bet you were really worried about me, Robby. And yes I know about your dad and Gramps . . . a real shocker all right. Marge Wainright, the night manager of Bar 31, called to give me the awful news. I contacted Cappecio's Funeral Home to make the arrangements. Their bodies are being cremated. I'll be home in a few hours. Love Ya." Mom abruptly hung up.

Leave it to Mom to wrap up this tragedy and put a ribbon on it. It's as if she is sweeping this part of her life under the rug. There's no consoling, no grieving, no crying, no muss, no fuss.

I know I'm young, immature, haven't lived much, haven't experienced many hardships, but I know life is not meant to be trivialized.

This is my biological father and Gramps we are talking about, not some distant dirt bags we don't care about.

I took a deep breath; suddenly in the midst of this horrible tragedy I found strength from within even though filled with some anger from my mother's devil-may-care behavior.

I knew in our tight-knit community there would be a few people who would come to the funeral home; some of my crowd I could associate with; some who would express their heartfelt feelings about my loss.

I fell asleep with some of these desperate feelings of despair falling away. Mom said she would be home in a few hours. As of 3:00 AM when I got up to go to the bathroom, she hadn't come home yet.

The light at 6:00 AM blinded me. I showered, went into the kitchen, saw a note on the table: "Hello, Robby, put your dark suit on and get to Cappecio's by 10:00 AM. Your aunt and I already made all the arrangements. After the service we're going to Sigmans—Love ya, Mom.

What is this, a friggin' party? Aunt Sophia is more of a flirt than Mom. Suddenly my mind was sped up and reeling again. My stomach churned, my head ached, and I detested this day and what it might bring.

My dark suit, I say black, my Johnny Cash outfit. Mom says dark blue. It was rumpled and smelled musty to me. Where was my Gibson guitar, my back to the audience—and down I go into a burning ring of fire.

Cappecio's sits at the apex of uptown and downtown, at the corner of Forest and Main, a third-generation death house and keeper of dead souls, but only temporary until they exited stage right to the Richville Cemetery of Eternal Rest and Enshrinement.

I know the Cappecio family personally; everybody worked in the business from Papa Reggio to Mama Adelaide and their kids Guido and Maria. I had a crush on Maria in the ninth grade. She was short, squat with hunching shoulders and duck-like feet, but she was built like the old brick outhouse in the Richville Township Park.

Guido, a thirty-something, grizzly-looking, hairy, pock-faced male who looked to be much older always had a blank, vague, expressionless demeanor. He had seen too many of our high school students drink too much brew and drive off Ridge Road into gullies, ditches, and down onto embankments where the array of mangled car and trunk parts would make any junk yard entrepreneur proud.

Over the last three years alone, ten of our high school's finest met their tragic demise along this menacing asphalt jungle.

Oh, I forgot, Marv Sweeny and Leod Bollier met their final fate while jumping the tracks at thirty-one mile and Piney Road. Their Chevy with the Hemi engine flipped and sailed off onto a side road by the Richville filtration plant.

Then there was Billy Weber who was wearing a headset when struck by a Great Truck local barreling through that same intersection. The Cappecio family fit Billie's body together like some anatomical jigsaw puzzle, except I'm sure certain cranial parts were missing—enough said.

Entering Cappecio's through a stain-glassed gold-arched double door into a hallway, I looked for the sign Andrew Criten Sr. and Andrew Criten Jr.

A lady comes toward me. and I recognize her as Mr. Rory Reign's wife, Millie. He is the town's eminent entrepreneur and is rumored to want to start a funeral home just outside of town by the Richville Water Tower, land he recently purchased from the township.

"I'm sorry for your loss, Rob. Everyone is gathered in viewing room four down the hall to your left," she motioned with her left hand.

My mother spots me; she and Sophie are standing in some form of reception line greeting grieving visitors. I recognize many people from Bar 31, various swamp scum, alcoholics, beer guzzlers, druggies, and just plain losers with whom my mother associates. "Over here, Robby. Stand in line like a good boy; you need a haircut, son. Why is your suit all rumpled? And your shoes not shined? That peach fuzz of yours has actually sprouted stubble—you should think about shaving," she went on.

"You know your Aunt Sophia. At least you should. Don't we look like twins in our weeping outfits? Black is in for these occasions, Robby; too bad your rumpled suit is dark blue, not the grieving kind."

"My, my so this is Robby, all grown up and no place to go. I hear you're havin' trouble at school, quit your job, and just—what's the term, sis—hangin' around. Aren't we the self-centered little man." Aunt Sophia babbles on and on, "A shame, a dirty shame Andy and his dad . . . poof up in smoke . . . closed casket . . . a tragedy, but oh how they were cool when they smoked their joints, so mellow, a couple a mellow fellows . . . ." Would Sophia not stop bellowing these impulsive thoughts to all around who cared to hear? And most wanted to! I turn and see Maria, and my mind wanders to wanting to ravish her . . . so near, yet so far.

Oh crap, here comes Mom's latest leech lover, a guy she met in church. My mother has no limits—she sees no shame in preying by praying. This latest wonder is a born-again Christian who was dunked in the Belle River by a Pentecostal preacher. This dude was held under water a record sixty-eight seconds, surfacing with the light of Calvary shining from his blue-crystal eye sockets. Barf, barf, barf.

His name is Billy Sweetwell. He was just passing through Richville when Mama bagged this buffoon.

I turn my head away as he gives Mom a big, erotic, let's-do-it-standing-up hug. She screams with delight and says, "You've straightened my vertebrae and given me a massage at the same time."

"You're my wench lady and man that black lacy garment you call a dress makes me want to complete my born-again mission right here and now—I can feel my loins a movin'," Mr. Sweetwell bellows in Mom's ear, but for all to hear.

Our crazy cast of characters assembles and waits for Reverend Heuther to preside over this memorial service.

I am seated in the front row. I hear noises in the back of the room and see some Richville High School students. Five seniors sat next to each other in the last row. Dana McElvy, the banker's daughter, Matt Flarety Mr. Everything, Jim Thomas, a nice jock, Scott Menage a real go-getter and Stacey McDonald, the beauty queen and all-around high school sweetheart. What are they doing here at this circus-like freak show? Here comes Dana. What does she have to say? Maybe she'll just give her condolences to my mom.

"Rob, Rob." I came out of my daze. "The gang would like to talk to you after the service, okay? Here comes Reverend Huether. Don't leave after the service."

I stuttered some vague phrase, "Good to see you. I won't leave—where would I go anyway?"

The reverend steps up behind a podium. He taps the mic. A screeching, blaring sound emits; everyone is startled. Let this farce begin.

Suddenly the lighting in the room flickers and the microphone emits a staticky sound shrill enough to scare away the entire canine population of Richville. Leave it to the Reverend, not known for his speaking ability, to really screw this service with a power outage.

The Reverend gains our attention by looking upward toward the ceiling and beginning his eulogy: "Heavenly Father we are gathered here to praise you and give you thanks for saving our souls and giving us your grace in this hour of need. We pray for the souls of Andy and Andy Jr. who have perished in a deadly inferno of the Devil's making.

"Praise the family here today for their enduring strength and love of Andy and Andy Jr.

"I say to you who are seated here today, grieve not my brothers, be healed. We are all flawed; we fall and fail. Each of us, with knowledge or without, contributes to the suffering around us, if not with forethought, then by our pretense of innocence, comfortable condemnation, and arrogance. When these frailties are relinquished, all becomes right in thought and action. Therein lies everyman's sacrifice and his salvation as well.

"Praise God from whom all blessings flow, praise all creatures here below, praise Father, Son, and Holy Ghost. Amen."

The service ends and I feel a tap on my shoulder. It's Dana. "Come back to school; you are certainly missed. I sense the problems with your family have kept you out of school."

The rest of the group suddenly assembles around me. Each student expresses their condolences, each was heartfelt in their remarks.

Jim Thomas issues me a challenge. "Come back, finish the school year. Tad 'The Man' Reeves, our fellow hero who died of cancer, mentioned your name when he and the others talked about us seniors climbing Richville's Water Tower at the end of the school year.

"For some unknown reason no one approached you. We're truly sorry. Come back in his name, finish your senior year, put your mark on that tower," Jim encourages me.

The others nod in agreement. My cheeks redden. I am confused . . . all this attention at once.

I see Mom, Aunty, and Sweetwell looking at me, I think with disdain. They want me to vacate the premises and hurry over to Sigman's where their party will really begin.

Mom speaks for the group. "Maybe one of your classmates here can give you a ride to Sigman's. We're outta here." Billy just glares at me, and Aunty is busy adjusting her low cut black dress, showing her ample cleavage in the Reverend's direction.

Reverend Huether comes over and expresses his condolences. Before Mom leaves, the Reverend hustles over and the two exchange dialogues, which allude to an envelope with a few dollar bills in it as payment for the services of the Reverend. "Not nearly enough" I heard the Reverend utter, his face crimson and eyes glaring at Mom.

I tell the group I'll consider coming back to school, yet I doubt Tad mentioned my name with regard to climbing the water tower.

Dana mentions one last thing. "When you do come back, see Mr. Winkow the counselor. I spoke to him about you and your entertaining ways. He claims to have some information on scholarship programs at the Spitzer School of Broadcasting.

Instead of attending the alcohol-infested bash at Sigman's, I go back to my dark, depressing, rat hole of a room.

The decision to return to school is not an easy one. I re-enroll the following Monday and talk to Mr. Winkow. He fills me in on the broadcast school, and I sign up for a tour of the facility later in the school year.

As for climbing the water tower, I am determined to help out any way I can and will meet with my fellow seniors to discuss the whys and wherefores of the tradition.

Can I say I have overcome my depression? Can I say I've moved away from those dark recesses, those scary times in my mind when all seems lost? No. A thousand times no.

My mom and her meandering devious ways will always haunt me. Her constant naysaying, badgering, and put-downs are a constant threat to my homeostasis and balance.

I know I must endure and leave my environment and find a new life for myself elsewhere. I must make it through the school year, then make my move to that broadcasting school.

Why my fellow students took an interest in me I'll never know. I knew about this Tad Reeves character; bigger than life. He knew at the beginning of his senior year he had brain cancer. He died the following spring. I knew he and Dana were a couple, but I was always on the outside of that group and most groups at Richville high school.

For all my antics and attention-getting, self-centered behavior, I was a loner, a person consumed by my own self-loathing and self-hatred.

Maybe the Reverend or what he said was right; I was contributing to the suffering around me by adding to it. I was condemning everyone else and not really seeing any good within myself—how arrogant of me.

It shouldn't have taken the deaths of my own flesh and blood to reveal these truths to me. I keep my father and grandfather's persona in my thoughts every day.

I supposed I can say I may rise from my own ashes and begin a new life somehow, somewhere down the road in the not too distant future.

Only time will tell. I now believe we can overcome our shortcomings and can make something of our young lives.

My story had only started. Back to chapter one. You, my fellow listeners, have come into my life. Watch me rejuvenate and move forward as we all have to.

I have heard time waits for no man or in my case adolescent young man. Thanks for being a part of my never-ending story.

Bless you fellow students for each making your own trail and pathway in your own lives. Each of us is an individual capable of going to good places we never thought possible.

Let our journeys through adulthood begin now where we can write our own scripts to succeed in our own positive way.

Thank you again for coming into my world to witness my pathway from depression and out of no man's land to possibly a brighter future into the light of day.

The Cartlotto Family Gravel Pit

Summer Tragedy Looms

Let this journey begin.

Several hundred youth over the course of the summer would be drawn to the Carlotto Family gravel pit, a place just outside of town off a back road along the family's acreage.

Now abandoned, "The Pit," as it is referred to by all who know about it, is a circle-shaped, dug-out pit thirty to thirty-five feet deep at its deepest.

The water is a deep blue color and sparkles brightly in the summer sun. This pit, while inviting youth to skinny dip, is actually a dangerous, deadly, and chilling-to-the-bone, a potential death trap for all who enter.

Thus the fascination and the lure. Despite the warning signs (literal)—absolutely no trespassing; stay out of area; no hunting in area; no swimming; abandoned pit dangerous—and figurative— "This is just a stupid place to put your carcass"— Richville's youth paraded year after year to this so-called rural Cancun in the northern woods.

Richville and surrounding towns' police forces patrolled the area, wrote tickets, and took a handful of these summer youth to the slammer for the night but in no way discouraged the massive throng of visitors each summer.

The Carlotto family was fined and told to drain the pit, fill it in, and cover it over since it was abandoned. They complied but said it would be one more summer before this would take place—one more summer of fun for these daring youth to "do their thing at The Pit."

Thus, the infamous Tower Gang of the Five decided collectively to challenge the senior class of Burrville High School to some type of contest to be held at The Pit over the Fourth of July weekend.

This had to be done with a great degree of discretion, even secrecy, lest certain adults and the law would intervene to squash this effort at just having fun.

The word went out to a group called the Burrville Bunch, a group of seniors who would comply with the directions and rules coming from The Tower Gang of Five.

It was decided that each group would construct five small floatable containers to be raced lengthwise on the Pit. Whichever group won three of these races would be declared the victor.

A victory cup would be presented to the leader of the winning team. The two schools would certainly party the rest of the day into the evening this July 4th weekend in this the last year the Pit would have any life, soon to be filled in to become, in time, a distant memory of good times past.

A week before the event, the Tower Gang of Five visited the Pit to go over last minute arrangements.

Unbeknownst to these teens, they were being watched from a wooded area only a few yards from The Pit; a forty-something-year-old, stooped-shouldered, bedraggled-looking figure of a man who, with a pockmarked face and permanently sour expression on this face, looked to always be the one who cast doubt on any individual or proceedings where he thought the parties to be up to "no good".

With his dart-like glance at these teens, his stomach churned, his mind quick as ever, and his temper turning to rage, he continued his surveillance of these interlopers into his private world.

His name Malcomb Baldridge. His family in the annals of Richville history go back three generations when his great-great-grandfather Mudgy came to create a life for himself and his family.

It was reported that Mudgy was either a renowned but repugnant scam artist of the era and area or one of the unluckiest people ever to settle in the community of Richville.

Upon three years of arriving, his home was mysteriously burned to the ground, a payback perhaps of a debt he owed to a nearby mob.

Mudgy went into the hotel business with other bankers, but within a year, again, the hotel was burned to the ground.

Did Mudgy burn it down to collect the insurance money? Perhaps. Other business ventures failed; the antique business where he was accused of ransacking area homes and stealing everything from tiffany lamps to horse hair chairs to Cherrywood armoires to gold-lined caskets at the Harbor Rest Funeral Home was a particularly festering story of intrigue and foul play.

Never brought to justice for these alleged crimes, he and his family lived as transients in the small towns that dotted Richville.

Malcomb, now the great-great-grandson, inherited a penchant for "playing the scam artist," only more in a white collar way. Malcomb served time at the county and state prisons for bank fraud and operating as the front man for a Ponzi scheme fleecing mostly the older, hardworking residents of Richville out of their retirement savings.

As he is now harbored in his forested hideaway, the vast population of Richville know his whereabouts but don't really care what this ne'er-do-well was doing nor his location away from the town's major population center.

Let him live out his final days a lonely, broken man most would say. Some would echo that his soul could be saved, but Malcomb or "Mac," as he was called in his earlier years, would have to make the first move toward his salvation.

Once Reverend Heuther made the trek out to his cabin in the woods and was met with a shotgun reception, the sign at the end of the driveway on a tall rotted post read, *I shoot and ask questions later*. So much for this attempt to draw on more congregant back to the flock.

Malcomb's peering eyes at these reckless teens that week before the race at the Pit could only spell disaster.

Malcomb was known as "Mac the Smack" in his earlier pugilistic years; that plus a fondness for guns could lead up to a troubling weekend for the teens. The police would certainly not be around The Pit that weekend unless by a miniscule of a miracle; the Richville Police department would most likely be at the annual "Our corn knee high by the Fourth of July festival" at Billings Gate Park.

The day of the event arrived. Even the tower group was surprised by the secrets that were not revealed; no tattling, not even a rumor got out into the public domain.

By midmorning the sun was blazing, and the bank thermometers skyrocketed to the hundred-degree mark (we know this was not an accurate measurement, but the temperature was scorching nevertheless).

At Billingsgate Park people arrived early and set up their wares under the recently-built shelter by the gazebo.

The town fathers would be there at high noon to bless the day and the event and to remind the populace of Richville about the first Remembrance of Good Days Past coming to Richville the week after Labor Day.

It was surprising even to these optimistic town leaders how many volunteers had come forward to help plan their part in the upcoming festivities.

Even surrounding communities wanted to participate by entering their fruits, vegetables, and prime animals for judging and by including high school bands and cheerleaders for marching and even adding floats of their own—mostly advertising their businesses, but nevertheless in a giving sharing way.

The regions' politicians wanted to walk the route to display their stamina and staying power to represent their constituents. When one regional political leader stepped forward, others followed.

There would also be several riding groups represented, decorating their horses with bespeckled bridles, saddles, and other ornate creations.

There would be ten area Knights of Columbus groups marching with their plumed hats and regalia.

The Knudson clan convinced the original Sons of the Viking Mist group to fly from Lappland to Richville to march in the parade. Petr Knudson was especially proud to have his Swedish heritage recognized at this first parade.

At The Pit, the two schools set up their own version of summer fun. Blankets were placed on the graveled ground along with coolers filled with liquid refreshment.

The Richville Tower of Five group and the Burrville Bunch brought along their constituent group to root their school on to victory.

Jim Thomas introduced himself and his members to the other team and bid the contest to start. Two participants, one from each team, would race in a handmade floating raft from one end of the pit to the other. The best three of five heats would be declared the victor; then let the real sun-drenched hoopla Fourth of July celebration begin.

Matt Flarety and one of the Burrville Bunch were first. Matt was beaten by an eyelash as he removed himself at the south end of the pit, exhausted but drenched from the cold, icy water. Scott Menage, who crafted a hollowed out dingy-like raft, beat his opponent. Jim Thomas, Mr. all-sports stud at Richville High School, lost a close match to Scott Belander, his equal at Burville High.

Stacey McDonald paddled her way to victory in what was a runaway race. The crowd on the bank of the pit on the opposite side knew what was coming. Now the air of anticipation was very tense; the cheerleaders who came began their chants, "Stand up, sit down, fight, fight, fight. The Richville Blue Devils show their might, might, might."

One Burrville cheerleader screamed, "Lean to the left, lean to the right, the Burrville Bulldogs will fight fight fight."

Dana McElvy crafted a six-foot long paddleboard coming to an aerodynamic curve at the tip. She had hid this board from her family by stashing it in their old barn behind their farmhouse. Now she would paddle the full length, a football field, north to south to lead her team to victory on this piercingly bright, sweltering, summer Fourth of July in her nineteenth year of life in this most beloved place, Richville.

The Burrville team countered with their own Wunderkind female star athlete, Ashley Montague, a three-star varsity athlete.

On your mark, get set, go. With much gusto, both girls were off and paddling. Now the roar of the crowd was deafening, each side urging these last two participants on to victory.

Even more important than a mere trophy, bragging rights were at stake. The two small rural schools were vying for prestige, glory, and honor for their senior class to be handed to the incoming senior class.

The glare of the afternoon sun now made the water appear as diamonds and sparkling gems. Spectators shielded their eyes to strain and witness this last race.

Something was wrong, however. Viewers could only spot one racer; the other board was without a driver.

Now chaos and panic overtook these youth. From both sides of the pit, they ran closer to the water, peering out to try and make some sense of the moment. Were their collective eyes deceiving them?

The Burrville paddler was on her craft now almost to the finish line while the Richville craft bobbed aimlessly on top, now being blown toward the shore on the east.

Dana McElvy was nowhere to be found and was possibly now sucked under the surface by the undertow and ever-changing currents in The Pit. Also, the water becomes bitter, ice cold the deeper one plunges in its depth, causing cramping and nausea.

No one youth jumped in the frigid water to begin the task of combing the depths. It appeared Dana may have fallen off in the middle of the Pit, about fifty yards from the finish at the south end.

Suddenly from the dark forested area east of The Pit emerged a stooped figure with a full white beard cascading to his waist, dressed in bib overalls, a red flannel shirt, and bare of feet.

Before the crowd could react, this stooped figure plunged into the icy depths, disappearing as stunned onlookers stood frozen on their respective sides of The Pit.

Jim Thomas did wade into the water; the drop-off came quick and seemed to swallow him up.

This strange foreigner of a figure emerged after what seemed to be several minutes with a lifeless body—Dana McElvy.

He proceeded to administer CPR; the crowd around him seeming to creep up suffocating his movement.

"Get back, you crazy punks, give this lady room to breathe. You stupid animals should know better than to play here. You numbskulls aren't good at reading warning signs," the bedeviled man uttered after the first series of CPR moves was performed.

After a few minutes Dana gasped, spit out water, and was looking up at this elderly man who came from nowhere to save her life.

Trying to adjust to the searing sunlight, Dana looked up and uttered, "Where am I, what happened? Did our team win the race?"

The man rose and looked at the crowd of onlookers—over fifty youth about to party on in this most dangerous of places—and bellowed, "Get out of here—never come here again. Next time I'll have my Winchester to greet you.

"You stupid jerks should be with your parents and family at the park in Richville and you Burville punks should just go home where you belong. And you're supposed to be the *leaders* of your classes," the growling man went on a rage.

A few of the throng thanked him; most started for their cars to leave The Pit area. Dana only said, "I was sinking deeper and deeper; that pit didn't seem to have a bottom. I couldn't get going back and my legs were cramping bad."

Within seconds this man was gone back to his forested man-made cabin in the woods. The crowd dispersed. The Tower Five and their group vacated the area. The Burrville group never gloated or proclaimed victory; they also departed the scene far more cautiously and meekly than when they had arrived.

No one made a move to go into those woods to confront the man who saved Dana's life. Who was this man and where had he come from?

Maybe fate had intervened that day to save Dana McElvy's life. She now, in her young life, had two death-like experiences—one taking Tad's life and one almost her own.

She was growing up fast, perhaps too fast. Had she just jumped into the adult world where life seemed more serious and darker?

Pre-Festival Buzz

Over the remaining part of the summer she would busy herself in the many activities and committees to prepare the town for the first annual Remembrance of Good Days Past Richville Has Time For You festival. She would meet the many people who settled there in Richville and would discover the many layers of history reminiscent of those communities that have a rich textural past and where individuals have meshed together over generations to create a patchwork, a true melting pot, that carries the community to new heights and to future glory.

Richville was on the verge of glory. The town fathers and other citizens took a backseat to no other place in the region.

It was now up to Mayor Mervin LeRoy to bring this festival together and to put the community of Richville on this road to greater glory. Who or what could stop this momentum? Everything seemed to be in alignment for this festival to succeed beyond even the expectations of the town fathers. What could possibly be a stumbling block holding up the proceedings for a smooth initial first Remembrance of Good Days Past festival?

The garden club members put together ideas for a float in the parade. The club, proud of their efforts to grow and crossbreed many types of roses, wanted to find a place to display these floral beauties. They were especially proud of their efforts at hybridization, developing a grandiflora called the Queen Elizabeth; others in the club preferred the salmon-pink Sonia. The whole group agreed that the tea rose was too common and mundane. Their excitement about showing their achievements further sparked enthusiasm about the entire festival.

Petey Snodgrass was busy putting together an overall history of Richville going back as many as four generations. He discovered the families and characters who came and settled in Richville were a testament to the character and determination of these people who overcame hardships in their efforts to keep their families intact, have them educated, and to earn a living in this region.

The Gobbel brothers, Mathew, Mark, Luke, and Mosha, challenged anyone to bring to the festival any better produce to be judged by the county's agricultural extension department and the local grange organizations.

Nelly, Cooky's wife, began organizing a contest for desserts, which would range from pies to cookies to specialty desserts. She was always in the process of trying to improve her doughy jelly-filled concoction and said she would have it perfected by festival time. "Just give me the blue ribbon and trophy now!" (see addendum for winners of Jam, Jelly, preserve contest)

Cooky told her to cool it before she drove away customers with her smarty pants talk.

The Knudson family was busy with their own enterprises. Petr was writing to his Lapplander friends about the history of the Sons of the Viking Mist and was trying to inquire as to the proper regalia to wear, especially when walking proudly in the parade that Sunday.

Petr had learned also that a new very hearty and vibrant Christmas tree was making its presence known in the area and would be for sale at other lots during the season.

This Norway spruce grew taller, could withstand many possible diseases, and lasted much longer before the needles dried and fell off.

"Never would I grow this tree in my nursery!" Petr would bellow out this dictum to his neighbors, friends in Richville, and to his competitors.

"My douglas firs and various pines I am stocking will crush this new tree back into the earth where it deserves to rot and fade away." He would go on to anyone who would listen to these bellicose meanderings.

There were many, many inquiries about other activities taking place at this first festival. The phones rang off the hook at city hall with Mayor Mervin LeRoy and his city hall festival committee on the receiving end.

A group wanted to show their horses in a dressage demonstration and possibly a competitive jumping event.

Even Heine Manoosh, the feisty mayor of Burrville, wanted to initiate a cabbage competition by inviting any interested participant to "slaw it up" and create any type of slaw using their ethnic heritage, ingenuity, desire to achieve a more perfect slaw or just to beat the Burrville crowd, which felt it had the best slaw in the region and could not possibly lose to any upstart homemaker—especially those living a boring, dull, day-to-day, hum-drum life . . . namely those overly-settled citizens of Richville. The challenge from Heine and his chamber group was on. Burrville would even donate some of their varieties of cabbage for the contest.

After all, Heine was purported to have stated, "The dull citizens of Richville don't know what the term brassica really means. Alas, we who have this great knowledge of growing cabbages correctly over the years have already overcome the many pests that tend to invade these fields—root maggots, cut worms, cabbage worms, and the most vehement of diseases, blackleg." The challenge was thus thrown out to Richville.

Choir director Lou Fazzini challenged other choirs around the region to a "Good Old Time Father with Melodies Spiritual Harmony" contest—a title that would surely be shortened. He contacted a group, the Guardians of Harmony, to help him put together this competition.

The original festival committee was energized by this movement, but these contests had to be firmed up; the time and places of the events had to be scheduled. Mary Goldbrick took charge of the parade and lining up the floats, area bands, and groups to march as well as getting the permits and dealing with any other obstacles that might crop up.

Rapid Rory Reigns, ever the entrepreneur, began to license and put into production shirts to sell, key chains, and pot holders with the town clock logo along with Remembrance of Good Days Past. He received permission provided half the proceeds went back to support future festival activities.

This second week in July was especially muggy with temperatures topping the 100-degree Fahrenheit mark. Main Street was teeming hot with store owners trying to stay cool with fans, cross ventilation, and buying ice to wrap in towels to place on their brows. Nothing seemed to be working.

This main street ran for two and a half miles in an angular route southeast to northwest. Over a hundred and fifty years previous, farmers brought their slaughtered animals to market along the pathway.

Eventually a railroad line went along a track where a grain elevator, a slaughterhouse, an open market, and the town's first boarding house/hotel horse and buggy stop stood.

This convenient convergence of commerce rep-resented the first location in which the town expanded; the road was lengthened and eventually connected to other towns in the region.

The road at first was just dirt, mud and rutted. With the advent of the automobile, this road was widened and paved several times, but the recent wear and tear from the big Peterbilt and other trucks cluttering up traffic caused the cement to crack and the pavement to buckle in many places. Now chunks of concrete caused many a car and truck to puncture its tires and blow out their undercarriages. It became a liability to the city in the form of lawsuits, pending litigation, and threats by the automobile and trucking association of the region who asked the county's commissioners to "do something or else".

Combine this wreckage with the damaged, clogged sewer system and the constant flooding—the town itself was after all in a valley—and this mess was magnified even more.

This morning in July only eight weeks from festival time with most of the details worked out, the town eager to participate, the events scheduled and ready to go, the mayor and city manager sat solemnly in a small room with the county's road commissioner and the town's political representative to the county's board of commissioners.

The meeting only lasted about ten minutes. After the officials left, Mayor LeRoy was left to talk to the newly-appointed city manager Myron Proudfoot, a man half the age of the veteran politician; however, both men just stared at each other numb and dumbfounded by the decision of the county's road commissioner.

"How can the main street of town be shut down until major repairs are made?" the new city manager echoed this harsh decision, his face somber and his boyish feature contorted in some form of agony.

"All the traffic will be rerouted around town; the parade is all but history now. There is no other route to take. Our goose is cooked," the mayor exclaimed with a look of forlorn defeat on his older, wiser, but now defeated-looking face.

He went on, "We have no time to make these major repairs; the county has used up its funds for the year with other projects.

"As of next Monday, four days away, our citizens will be told Main Street will be blocked off, our businesses screwed to the gills, no parade, I'll be hung, and you, my fine feathered friend, will also be hung out to dry on your first month in office." The mayor, now sweating profusely, felt trapped in a time and place he did not want to be.

"I have no options. Could we have fixed this road in years past? Should we have? Certainly. Is this debacle really all my fault? The citizens of Richville, as forgiving as they are, will surely pin the blame on me," he said, now with tears falling down onto his cheeks.

The new city manager left abruptly to ponder his next career move. The mayor sat in his high back plush leather chair, pondering *his* next move, perhaps to be exiled to his own Bonaparte-like island of Elba.

As day moved into night, another warm summer evening emerged in Richville. With the sounds of the cicadas, the crickets chirping, a summer concert beginning in Billings Gate Park, happy active youth playing sandlot ball, and a young couple vowing their love for each other by making their mark on the Loving Rock, Richville was in its summer glory; no other place on earth seemed more perfect. Tonight the stars would shine down over the town, blanketing it with a shining light to match the perfection of the heavens above.

Mayor LeRoy sat locked in his office with an order not to be disturbed. The disruption the following Monday caused by the barricades and the loss of revenue for the business community would be irreparable. How, too, would the town council address this problem? Where, indeed, would the money come from to repair the damaged street? The general fund was almost depleted, the sinking fund had sunk to a new low. It would take months to put a vote to the people to float a bond proposal, and lawsuits against the trucking industry would take time, be very costly, and would be futile anyway.

The mayor put his head down on the long council table and fell asleep. His family, at home, would surmise this was just another late night of meetings, meetings, meetings, though he had not called to tell any family member when he would actually be home.

At dawn he was awakened by a pounding on the council chamber door. "I know you're in there, old man," came an abrupt cry.

Oh great the mayor thought, word has leaked out. Now I'm a goner. This nightmare will be worse than being tarred and feathered. I've nowhere to run. My own political goose is cooked.

"Open up, LeRoy. I've got a message for you," came another terse reply.

The voice was not harsh, only abrupt. "It's Dean Beanie calling—do I have to bust down the door?"

With that last retort the mayor unlocked the door. Dean Beanie entered, his usual bank-like formal countenance preceded his urgency to talk to the mayor. The mayor relented and bid the banker to sit and spill out the bile, which certainly the mayor knew was coming.

Dean Beanie only said in his usual low key banker's voice, "Wait until I tell you about the business I just transacted."

Maybe, thought the mayor, the rotten truth hasn't hit the fan yet; it'll just give me more time to squirm and it'll make the noose tighter around my political neck.

The Dean continued, "We know about the tragedy on Main Street. You can't suppress a problem like that even for a day around our small community.

"As president of the Richville Bank, I get many proposals for new business ventures every day. This morning, I entertained a visitor who came to the bank in an unusual disguise and gave an envelope to one of our tellers then quickly vanished! He wishes to remain anonymous. Needless to say, this visitor cut a check in an amount big enough to repair the street and put everybody back in business again." Dean uttered this in his usual matter of fact manner.

"Further, the Carlotto Family will be contracted to pave the street and make all the necessary repairs. They will sub-contract any other work that needs to be done."

The mayor had prayed for a miracle, but he was a pragmatic politician and knew that miracles were seldom if ever a reality in the rough and tumble world of politics.

"I don't understand what is happening, but for once maybe I can't control this scenario. This is too much to comprehend. You, Beanie, take this act of generosity from Mr. Anonymous and run with it." The mayor managed to utter these words with some of his composure returning.

Then Beanie further stated succinctly, "The street will, in fact, be closed for about two weeks—barricades will be up. But the Carlottos are well-respected by the county road commission and will have the job up to code and completed with five or six weeks left before the festival date."

The Road to Perdition

Is All Lost?

For the first time in Mayor Mervin LeRoy's peripatetic political career, he would step back, be a sidewalk superintendent to these proceedings, will not meddle, will not give his two cents worth of sage advising, and will not—when the project is completed—give any speeches commemorating "the event." He would stay calm, cool, collected, and out of the way—maybe he would go to Cooky's Café when the job was almost complete. He would figuratively "bite his tongue," be thankful for this miracle of miracles, and just be as humble as his political self can be. He did wonder (put these thoughts aside) for a moment who this anonymous donor was and what, if anything, did he or she want in return.

He needed to meet with the festival committee that following Monday the third week in what was turning out to be a hot, humid ,and often stormy summer. He at least knew of one storm that was quelled. Though the town's businesses would be inconvenienced for a few weeks, the result would hopefully be a better more permanent safer roadway. Maybe eventually he would convince the truck driving union and their truckers. There were new roads scheduled to be built in future years heading north around Richville. Maybe the time table could be moved up. But for now he again could focus on the festival. The next meeting would take place in his council's chambers. Any problems now being raised concerning the festival would seem trivial compared with the road fiasco.

Main Street was closed for two and a half weeks as the Carlotto family subcontracted much of the repair work out to their vendors. Though the street businesses were interrupted, most were okay with the closing, as they realized the benefits of a newly paved street in the long run.

Meanwhile at the far reaches of Billings Gate Park, Barny Bard donated an old barn that was being rebuilt on the park property. This structure would be known as Ye Good Ole Red Barn and would be used as headquarters for the festival. During the festival day, arts and crafts, vegetables, plants, and other booths would fill up the structure.

During the rest of the year, it would serve as storage for the disassembled floats and machinery the festival would accumulate.

Missy Menage, the garden club president, was not happy with having the barn so close to the floribunda area. She claimed the barn, during certain times of day, cast shadows over the garden space thus depriving these flowers of much needed sunlight during the most intense growing time of the summer. "I will not move these gardens," she proclaimed. "In a few years we will be known as Rose City, and we will outgrow any other municipality who dares to challenge our claim."

Leave it to Petey Snodgrass Sr. to discover that Heine Manoosh, the "Cabbage King" mayor of Burrville, had relatives a century ago who settled just inside the then township limits of Richville.

They farmed the land for a few decades then moved out and were never heard from again. Petey surmised the family ingested poisoned water from a well they dug and were slowly poisoned to death. It was ironic they had started to grow cabbage on their land, but could not sell it.

Leave it to Heine to take up this labor and make it successful in his own town. Certainly the cabbage competition would be one of the highlights of this first upcoming Remembrance of Good Days Past festival.

The summer days in Richville rolled along. The Dog Days were hot, humid, and the community pool cooled many a Richville resident.

The summer softball league was in full swing with eight teams, one from Richville and seven others from surrounding towns, all vying for the coveted Super Softball Regional Little World Series trophy, a traveling trophy now over twenty years old. This league went back to the beginning of the depression era. The trophy itself was an amalgam of car parts melted together to form a large softball at the top with a chrome base. The winning team's name and year of their championship was welded on the side of the stanchion.

A committee formed to have these same teams compete in the first annual Remembrance of Good Days Past regional softball tournament to be held in Billings Gate Park.

The festival committee met at Cooky's in the month of August for the last time. Subsequent meetings would be held at the now fully reconstructed Ye Good Ole Red Barn.

Rapid Rory Reigns was busy creating a float for every one of his enterprises—the laundry, the movie theatre, and the golf course. He wanted to have his golf course employees march in the parade with golf club in hand; they could pick their own club and would be called the Hickory Stick Swingers. When word got around town, this was frowned upon and Rory would think twice about this idea. What kind of swingers would these people represent? The prudes in town would say to Rory under no uncertain terms.

A Confrontational Meeting in the Woods

The Banker Meets the Cranker

Mayor LeRoy just received confirmation that the JC Carter Perfect Performing Pleasures for Mind & Soul show would be contracted for the festival. They would bring their many rides and midway shows. They were purported to have the fastest circling merry-go-round, going one mile faster than a similar merry-go-round at a park in Akron, OH, of any traveling show.

Along with a ferris wheel and other rides, they would bring their own freak show; though they claimed it was more humane than other more vile shows. Apparently the fat lady was on some form of weight loss program and would be leaving the show when she lost a hundred more pounds.

The bearded lady was actually going through a sex change operation and would also bow out of the show and would be promoted to a manager of the midway very soon.

The JC Carter Organization paid these individuals handsomely and changed the term freak to "anomalies of nature—wonderments from above" in order to be more in keeping with the politically correct spirit of this often seedy business.

The three hundred or so volunteers for this first festival were in an organizational frenzy. All the flower, vegetable, baked, and canned goods competitions were sorted out. The winner would receive either a Grand Champion, blue, red, or white ribbon.

Leave it to Mary Goldbrick to want to add an honorable mention category. After all she, in her craft store, was responsible for all the ribbon making and she could charge a bit more to the festival committee for this extra prize, which kept some members of the volunteer crowd questioning her true motives.

Dean Beanie McElvy, president of Hometown Bank, discussed with a teller, Margerie McQuade, the envelope brought in by a large male, dressed in bib overalls with a hooded jacket covering his face. He just came into the bank, handed Margerie the envelope, and quickly retreated out of line and out of the bank.

Margerie initially thought this may be a robbery, but then that thought subsided as this hunched over disheveled looking stranger quickly exited from the premises.

Dean Beanie had also heard the rumors that a complete stranger, large in stature, long white beard hanging scraggly three feet or more from a pock-marked face, had saved his daughter from drowning in The Pit over the Fourth of July.

Dana never admitted any of this to her father, so it was left to the banker's logical inductive reasoning to solve this mystery and bring closure to the who, what, where, why— (leave out when) of the matter.

Dean went to this forested cottage of one Malcomb Baldridge, the supposed town malcontent and lover who was holed up for who knows how many years in that man-made forested retreat of his.

Dean went alone as he felt taking anyone with him would only stir up more of a ruckus. He knew Malcomb was armed—maybe dangerous, maybe not.

He set off, not telling anyone where he was going one morning when the ragweed caused the town's residents to sneeze in a collective outburst of snorting, hacking, wheezing, sniffling, and downright high decibel sounds, which rivaled the high pitches of a high school rock band discordantly interfering with one's own attempt to remain tranquil amidst all this decadent nonsense.

Dean approached the cabin with trepidation lest the area around it be booby trapped or Mr. Baldridge decided to unload his shotgun in the banker's direction.

There was no walkway just brush and leaves strewn about in front of the cabin. Dean made a beeline for the front door. He was about ten yards from the door as a loud booming voice called out, "Come any closer and you're a goner."

Dean stopped abruptly and called back, "It's you, Malcomb. I just want answers to two questions then I'll leave. I don't care why you're holed up here or what you or your family have done in the past—just answer me these questions."

"Make it brief, banker boy, then get off my property," the gruffness now coming out of Malcomb's voice.

"You saved my daughter's life, didn't you? I'd like to thank you personally. If there's anything I can do to help you or your family please let me know," Dean proclaimed, now thinking he could engage Malcomb in some form of dialogue.

Malcomb shouted back, "Your daughter and those other brats should have been at the park celebrating the Fourth with their parents and family, not playing deadly games at this pit. What kind of parent are you—you didn't know where your child was? Shame on you and the other parents. Now if you'll excuse me, Mr. Banker, I've got my own life to attend to. Kindly leave me alone."

Dean felt Malcomb slip away but had one more statement, not the question he was originally going to ask. "And thank you for saving the festival with that anonymous donation."

He thought he heard the clicking of a gun, or maybe the safety was being taken off. He carefully backed away and when he disappeared into the woods, he turned and ran toward his car parked on the other side of The Pit. Beads of sweat began trickling from his brow; his shirt was soaked in sweat. He realized this loner in the woods was still angry, but Malcomb was taking the brunt of the burden for generations of his family's mistakes, misgivings, and nefarious activities. Maybe at this point in his life, in his own way, he was giving back. At least, thought Dean, I tried to mend a fence here and there and tried to make contact with this man no one really knew, this isolate.

The banker left now with more questions than ever, but his mind was cleared somewhat as he at least made the attempt at communicating his thanks. So be it he said to himself. Let it rest. There is much work still to be done to insure that this festival would be a success.

Dean drove back to the bank. He would keep this meeting with Malcomb to himself.

Cooky Reflects on His Life at the Cafe One Last Time

Meanwhile at Cooky's Café, Cooky and Nelly finished another long day of serving quality food to newcomers and steady patrons who frequented the café.

For thirty three years, Cooky worked day and night to make his passion of cooking a success.

His first dollar was framed on a wall behind the cash register. Some of his original steel pots and pans were still in use. His large convection oven was fairly new; his walk in freezer was also purchased recently. Cooky felt he had to keep up with his competition in the area.

First a Chinese restaurant opened at the other end of Main Street, then a Greek restaurant just out of town on M19, then something called Coney Island Restaurant opened just a block away. Then, in an old stone block house (the manager lived upstairs) a German restaurant made its way to Richville.

Through all this, Cooky changed the décor, put in new booths and a spruced up counter, and experimented with a variety of cuisines. There was, however, always one factor that remained constant—the great quality of the food.

Cooky also put out great feasts for the homeless during the holidays and would cooperate with area churches, shelters, and food banks to bring in at least a hundred people for these festive dinners.

For a few years, Cooky had a catering business, but he lost money in this venture. He also partnered with a local bakery and always served the freshest rolls, breads, and pastries in the region. Nelly was always trying new variations on the bear claw, donut, or croissant much to the delight of patrons who frequented Cooky's Café.

His location at the corner of Main St. and Grand Ave. was the dividing line between what was called upper Richville and lower Richville. Cooky caught most of the traffic running north out of town. He also catered to the truckers, who were now more frequent in number, with big, fulfilling trucker's stew, big omelets, and masses of fried potatoes and other vegetables fresh in season from the Gobbel brothers farm. Cooky outlasted and out fought his competition with his charming ways and his ability to relate to the other mundane lives and daily hum drum behaviors of the common man. He made every customer feel a warm glow and felt that to come into Cooky's Café was to enter a special place.

Cooky believed in the people of Richville and took a special interest in the events that leave a mark on every common person, including special occasions such as birthdays, anniversaries, wedding announcements, babies being born, even those who have passed on. He knew how to console the grieving; his tender ways were appreciated by the area's clergy. Go to Cooky's if you want your soul, spirit, and stomach to be filled. "Glory be to all who enter these magical portals—you are a stranger but once" was the saying placed over the entranceway.

Cooky sat on a stool at the counter of the café. Nelly nervously paced around the diner, wiping down the tables and sweeping the floor. The lights were dimmed; the closed sign was on the front door.

"We'll be busy the week of Days of Remembrance. I hope we can stop long enough to see most of the parade passing by. We have the best view of any business; we're at the juncture where lower Richville goes into upper Richville.

"I'm glad someone saved the parade; I understand it was a benefactor with a lot of money. Thank goodness we have people like that here in our fair town," he said, rambling somewhat and Nellie, not looking up, didn't respond.

"This will be my first and last festival. Everything is happening so fast . . . decisions have to be made quickly . . . the sale of the café, my life put in some order.

"You Nelly will go on with your life. You have your church activities, the garden club, and all the close friends you've made here in Richville over the past thirty-two years. They'll support you. And our family, our two daughters and one son and their children, will all rally around you," said Cookie, continuing with his monologue, but Nelly now looked directly at Cooky, tears streaming down her face.

Nelly excitedly blurted out, "Why didn't those doctors, especially our family doctor, Dr. McMillan, find the cancer in time? Why didn't you get yearly checkups? Why did you never take time to relax, get away from this place? At times this restaurant seemed like a prison, solitary confinement with no escape. Why were you so good to the people here in this town? Why didn't you sell this place sooner and take better care of your health?" Nelly went on.

"And now you have a death sentence—no time to travel to those faraway places we'd planned to go. You're going to die having lived your entire working life in this small town café, with these small town people, many of whom are petty and filled with ill will. And you used up your energy treating them like kings and queens, as if they cared about you.

"You were rarely consulted about the big decisions that helped change this town."

"Stop this rant," Cooky interjected. "I did what I did because I honestly love what I do. And you know my love for the residents of this community.

"My time may be ending," he went on "but people will remember how we treated them. There will be many owners of this place who will come and go, but I had the staying power to make this business a success.

"Let's enjoy the time I have left. I will be alive for the festival; how long after . . . who knows," Cooky's voice now weak, his strength waning, his mind drifting off in a sleep-like mode.

"Let's go home—call it a day. You and Sammy [a loyal employee for the last ten years] take charge for the next few days while I rest." Cooky, now very exhausted, looked around the restaurant into which he put his life's work and sighed. He may not be able to work a full day again. Soon the people in Richville will know his fate.

And life will go on in Richville.

5/30/11

Final Details

Counting Down the Days

Meanwhile at the barn the mayor held court with last-minute details. The Reverend, superintendent, entrepreneur, and owner of the gift shop gave their final reports.

One of the town's residents, Norbert "Call Me the Rebel" Gibbon, filled in the mayor on his Civil War southern cannon, a replica of the big gun, and how he would fire it in the park to initiate the festival. This would happen right after the mayor's opening remarks to open the festival.

Norbert had to give his own story as to why he chose this particular cannon. "This giant cannon is the whistling Dick, so called for the whooshing noise it made as it was being fired."

"Yes, sir, this baby's an eighteen-inch smoothbore beauty. It was used most effectively at Vicksburg but then disappeared after the fall of Vicksburg and as history has it, it was dumped into the Mississippi River by Wyman Hill July 3, 1863."

He went on much to the chagrin of the mayor who had heard this story before and could quote it verbatim. "My great-great-great-granddaddy was there at Vicksburg, but we have no records as to whether he knew anything about where this great gun ended up."

"Anyway," Norbert finally summed up, "I'll be with you at the park with my baby; you won't hear a whooshing noise just a loud boom. Everyone within a mile ear shot will know the festival has started.

"Of course your opening remarks, mayor, will, I'm sure, cause my Rebel bones to shake with pride. I thank you for letting this old southern boy be in this northern town to start this festival.

He concluded, "I'll have this gun on display in this barn, well-guarded of course. I'd be glad also to tell anyone about the regiment I enact for the 119th South Carolina Rebel Mountaineers. And I'll be wearing proper garb also. I could bring my Yankee friend along Caleb Crabtree—we could really have a spitfire verbal battle. I think the festival goers would enjoy that."

"Okay, okay," the mayor relented now really tiring of Norbert's persistent rant.

The mayor surveyed the stalls for the arts, crafts, and winners of all the contests displayed.

He was pleased with all the progress and the way the volunteers had helped bring this first of its kind event to fruition.

The schedule of events had been completed and sent around the region a couple of months ago.

Press coverage would be at most of the events with five newspapers coming in to town this next week.

Now the mayor kept a careful eye on the weather. The early reports indicated above normal temperatures for the four days; no rain or inclement weather was in the forecast.

The residents of Richville and the region would now wait in anticipation.

Labor Day came and went and the week following seemed to plod along. That Thursday event in the park finally made its presence known.

The stage was set. By 6:00 PM the town notables were seated behind the mayor who paced nervously and stopped to tap the microphone as he uttered, "Attention, attention, residents of Richville."

The bleacher seats filled up fast with most of the three hundred or so volunteers, other major contributors to the festival, some contest participants, and the general public of Richville.

Lou Frazzini choir director of the Lutheran Church and an abbreviated number of choir members were there to sing and lead the National Anthem.

Norbert Gibbon was off the stage to one side in an open area ready to discharge the replica of the "Whistling Dick" cannon. He brought six rebel enactors who would "put the rebel screaming yell on these northern Yankees" and scare the pants and other articles of clothing off these northern ne'er-do-wells.

The press was present to record this first opening ceremony. They would remain throughout the week to catalogue the many events taking place throughout the grounds of the festival.

Again the mayor stepped to the microphone. He heard a catcall from the audience, "Make it short, I'm gettin' antsy sittin' on this hard bleacher."

Another voice cried out, "Hey, mayor, I ain't got no refrigeration for my vinegar coleslaw for the cabbage contest! I guess you messed that one up—nothin' like warm bacteria infested slaw."

Still another Richville citizen called out, "That barn you call home to all those contests and your offices is about ready to fall down in a dung heap. Who do you hire to get construction done around here?"

Again, a Richville citizen seemed to screech at the mayor, "Why is Barny Bard's great-grandfather the Grand Marshall? Yeah, he's a hundred and two, but long ago he bought Bard's Marsh and turned it into a hunting preserve, but his family shot most of the pheasant and duck and now the marsh is just a pile of weeds and mush."

The mayor held fast not responding to these invectives. Now it was his turn to speak. "Welcome, citizens of Richville, interested festival goers, participants in the many events and contests, and the many volunteers who put this first of hopefully many festivals together. We especially thank our board members Mary Goldbrick, Dr. DuVall, Reverend Harold Heuther, and Rapid Rory Reigns for their leadership bringing this festival to fruition.

"Now, Lou Fazzini will direct the Richville Lutheran choir in the singing of our national anthem." The mayor called out to the crowd to stand and sing.

"Now, Norbert Gibbon will fire off the whistling Dick cannon." The mayor turned toward Norbert. The sound reverberated throughout the park, out to the town itself, up M19, the other direction to the Hickory Stick Glen golf course, out to The Pit, over to Bard's Marsh, and over to the adjacent town of Burrville.

"Let the festival, Remembrance of Good Days Past begin!" The mayor was overcome with emotion, his demeanor bursting with pride and joy. All the frustrations, impediments, holdups, and blunders of the past few months now seemingly ancient history.

The crowd dispersed. The mayor, looking over the citizens, noticed the Gobbel brothers, Petey Snodgrass Sr., who would keep a diary of the events, and the Knudson family with a full complement of the Swedish society Sons of the Viking Mist.

The Carlotti family was present; thank goodness for their work to get the paving and restoration done on Main Street.

Dean Beanie McElvy gave the mayor the thumbs up sign. Missy Menage ran to the barn to complete the Miss Remembrance of Good Days Past float and the big rose float.

Dana Jansen McElvy was present with several students. They also prepared a float for the parade. Even Myron Proudfoot, the new city manager, was smiling even though he seemed shocked and overwhelmed by the turnout and town pride displayed by the citizenry of Richville.

Even Phil Dickerson, mayor of Reed Station whose own career as mayor was in jeopardy, was wide-eyed, his heart palpitating quickly. In the back of his mind he was jealous of Mayor LeRoy; how did such a bungling person put this together?

JC Carter himself of the JC Carter Perfect Performing Pleasures for Mind and Soul escorted the mayor that evening down the lighted midway. JC pointed out the merry-go-round brought to this festival was in fact the fastest in all of the United States, going sixteen miles per hour, one mile per hour faster than the race horse merry-go-round at a park in Sandusky, OH. The mayor thought, *more liability, just what I need*, but said nothing to JC.

The lights of the midway were very luminescent, multi-colored, and were all colors of the rainbow. J.C. pointed out these lights were in fact colors of the rainbow and the young festival goers could learn ROYGBIV—red, orange, yellow, green, blue, indigo, and violet. This was an educational experience also. The mayor only nodded halfheartedly.

The beer tent was called the entertainment arena even though there were twenty different beers sold from around the world. Various acts would appear in the tent as well as the harmony competition where Mr. Fazzini pulled together several singing groups from the area.

Ongoing at the barn were the contests, the biggest being the coleslaw contest. The coleslaw fare ranged from vinegar based, to honey, to Asian cabbage, to deviled egg, to Ramen noodles. Heine Manoosh and his entourage were excited to judge these entries. Heine, his ego often overtaking his sensibilities, backtracked and said he would not even think again of dumping cabbage remains in the Richville sewer system. He was receiving a great deal of publicity here at this neophyte festival for his own cabbage festival.

Rapid Rory Reigns busily hocked shirts, key chains, head bands, wrist bands, and hats with the Remembrance of Good Days Past logo on them and gave away free tickets to his movie theatre, two-for-one laundry coupons, and golf vouchers to the golf course. His floats would be in the parade.

Throughout the mayor's travels around the park and to the various events, he would spot what he thought was a large man in bib overalls with a long white beard. This man, at times, seemed to be an apparition darting behind trees and shrubs ever moving, here then there, then disappearing. Could it be . . . no, the mayor thought, *it's just my imagination.*

Cooky's Last Stand

A Triumph of Will and Skill

Meanwhile at Cooky's Café, the place smelled of fried chicken, golden French fries, fresh coleslaw, and those other encrusted whiffs of over thirty years of collected food entries into any foreign cuisine one could imagine.

Cooky hired several high school students, Dana McElvy among them, to serve the throng of festival goers.

Nelly, also present, baked those elephant-size claws—someone suggested the term pad as the correct word for an elephant's foot—but the verdict was still out as to what exactly these jelly-filled rolls should be named.

Cooky took to directing traffic as the horde of eager eaters descended on the café. Most remarked that Cooky's food was far superior in taste, portion size, and overall quality than the food found along the midway.

The long day ended with the Gobbel brothers Mathew, Mark, Luke, and Mosha gobbling up the last scrumptious plate of fried chicken.

"You're gonna have to leave this joint now, with your bellies full," Cooky called out to all the brothers. "Keep those fresh, fall vegetables you're harvesting coming in. I understand you're now in the egg business—I'll give it a try as long as they're fresh. My customers are to come first and they always know the quality of my food," Cooky concluded, turning toward the door to lock it.

Cooky sat down exhausted with nelly. "We'll have a great view of the parade Sunday—geez, I'm tired, pooped. Doc McMillan gave me the axe at the hospital. My tumor has spread to the big blood vessels; the superior mesenteric artery the main artery that comes off the aorta. Surgery is not possible . . . but you know that, too, don't you, sweetie. My fate is sealed.

"I love this place . . . doin' my job to the best of my ability for the folks of this town—the greatest folks and the best little town anywhere.

"The best food ever is being prepared for Sunday. The festival-goers can order what they want—the best steaks from local ranches, the best chicken ever, the freshest of vegetables and produce, and the best barbecue and sauce with my homemade blend of herbs and spices. I'm letting it all hang out, sweet pea." Cooky stopped and took a panoramic visual tour of his establishment.

Nelly sprang from her chair and the two embraced in a hug in which the warmth from both bodies ignited into each other, and the two felt the glow of love—a love from being married over forty years, having worked side by side at this diner for over thirty years, and from a pride of doing one's best in the day-to-day mundane atmosphere of Richville, where people come in to enjoy the food, the small cozy surroundings, and the positive spirit emanating from these owners (a job well done).

The Big Parade

Sunday morning came quickly. Almost all the activities were winding down. The festival barn was a flurry of activities. Phil Dickerson, mayor of Reed Station, won the slaw contest with his entry using several grades of vinegar and salad dressings. He called it "sour smash supreme."

The town notables gathered to check last-minute details for the parade. Everyone had to be in place at the upper edge of town, a couple of blocks from the mayor's barbershop, an hour or so before the start of the parade.

Maynard P. Bard was to be driven to the starting site. He was acting as feisty as ever—not a good choice for the role of Grand Marshall—but the mayor felt he was the logical choice, being the oldest known living resident of Richville, however sordid or soiled may have been his past.

"Piss on this parade," Maynard was alleged to have said. "I've got a hot date at my assisted living home—let's get this piece of crap done in a hurry."

Maynard detested putting on a suit and tie for any occasion and was purported to have a place in the 1800s and early 1900s where sheep were taken to slaughter.

Crowds four deep lined the streets along the route now eager for the first annual Remembrance of Good Days Past—We Have Time for You parade to start.

With every float, groups, and individuals in place, Mayor LeRoy gave the signal to begin. He hopped into the lead car, a 1934 Packard V12 convertible, with the Grand

Marshall Maynard P. Bard in tow. The other committee members fit into a 1937 Packard Super Eight automobile. It was not known whether these autos original or replicas, as they were donated by the family from Quad Motors, a semi-reputable used car company doing business in the region for over twenty-five years.

The parade participants lined up ready to revel in the glory of this first festival. The local Richville band paraded behind the front celebratory group. Then came the Sons of the Viking Mist with a mockup of a Viking ship and several members from Stockholm who made the trip just to pass on the traditions.

The Knudson family proudly waved the Swedish flag, with Petra and their children Johnny and Jeanny holding the Sons of the Viking Mist shield.

The Carlotto family followed with sons Billy, Jimmy, and Johnny holding up the family business sign reading "Carlotto rocks—none finer—but from us—avoid the fuss."

The JC Carter Perfect Performing Pleasures for Mind and Soul had many of its acts interspersed throughout the parade. The fat lady, tagged as the Rotund Butterball, was losing weight rapidly as she walked the entire route. She knew this would be her last hurrah of a parade as was slimming down to almost drastic proportions.

Missy Menage and her blooming Evervescent Rose Society put together a rose-like float and challenged other communities to "grow roses like us—or leaf us alone—we are number one in the rose growing business."

The Gobbel brothers followed with their own float, a long cart-like structure pulled by giant draft horses with a sign proclaiming their vegetables and fruits to be the purest and most wholesome, with more vitamins to the ounce than any other surrounding farm—Richville's finest. Mathew, Mark, and Luke were on the float smiling and waving to the crowd, throwing out occasional vegetable tidbits and a small recipe book with many of Mama Gobbels recipes in it. Mosha begrudgingly walked behind the cart shoveling waste from the horses into a large bin attached to the cart. This waste was to be recycled and used in the many experiments the Gobbel family undertook to reconstitute this excrement; nothing went to waste in the Gobbel family enterprise.

The many K of C units marched along the parade route. Decked in opulent-colored outfits with plumed fedoras and buckled shoes, these units provide a spit and polish shine to the parade.

Lou Fazzini, choir director of the Lutheran church, put together the gospel song fest and competition and was able to convince a number (five) area choirs to march and sing in the parade. "Onward Christian Soldiers" was the most popular song sung by the choir's parade goers with "Joshua Fit the Battle of Jericho" coming in a distant second. Lou would direct all these choirs at the park after the parade for the closing ceremonies and the singing of "Down in the Valley" as the final song to end the festival.

Dean Beanie McElvy bank president encouraged or forced his entire crew to march in the parade. Each marcher was immaculately dressed, the ladies smartly coifed in the latest chic style; no buns permitted. Participants could not wear glasses and this caused some walkers to bump into the walker ahead; one Ms. Molly Givens was nearly blind without glasses and drifted away from her procession and ended up on an adjacent sidewalk off the parade route.

Dean Beanie McElvy, the ever-present banker, public relation, and let's-not-be-stodgy politician thought glasses/

spectacles represented a bygone era in banking; let the cleaner, fresher more wholesome less stodgy look take over. The employees of the bank who wore these spectacles may have taken exception to the Dean's new PR campaign.

Dean Beanie, after all, was having problems with floaters and dots in front of his eyes. *Do as I say, not as I do* was Dean's request, as his own optician suggested he don spectacles to correct his 20-200 vision.

At the end of the parade was Norbert Gibbon and his fellow 119th South Carolina Rebel Mountaineers, pulling the replica of the whistling Dick cannon. Caleb Crabtree and the other rebel enactors yelled the rebel yell, ever drowning out the last band ahead of them from Burrville High School. They, too, would congregate in the park after the parade to be in the closing ceremony.

Sitting in his favorite armchair in front of his restaurant, Cooky had a panoramic view of the parade. By now every person in town knew of his terminal cancer.

Cooky sat stoically reminiscing over the past thirty years. To his right at the intersection of Main Street and the Grand Divide Avenue, he recalled how each day the Trunk Line train sped diagonally across the intersection, whizzing behind his restaurant at 4:00 PM and again the Midnight Special at 12:00 AM. The 4:00 PM train signaled the time the early bird special would begin. Usually the restaurant was packed with seniors this time of day. Many nights Cooky would be working past midnight and the special reminded him he should probably close his place for the day.

Each parade participant, as they passed the restaurant, gave a thumbs up and a hearty smile for Cooky to take in. Several paraders rubbed their tummies and mouthed the word yummy. That is except Maynard P. Bard who just looked straight ahead searching for the end of the parade route.

Passing Cooky's Café marked the passage of downtown Richville to the uptown section, which was more residential.

During the last half of the parade, Nelly came out from the busy restaurant to join her husband. "This seems like a tribute to you," she replied.

"I think you've fed every one of these parade-goers—you're food has been a staple in this town from early morning to late night," her eyes now misting.

Now thinking of his business again, Cooky remarked, "Have we sold all our ribs and chicken yet? That rib sauce was the very best—I keep special spices under lock and key. *You* don't even know where they are kept."

"It's all gone—every last morsel. This has been a very successful four days. We've done it again, love—food to fill the body and ignite the soul."

They embraced and kissed each other several times. The restaurant patrons and other onlookers burst out with a spontaneous applause. One exuberant onlooker shouted out "Bravo—bravo—job well done, you two."

The closing ceremony went well. Mayor LeRoy kept his remarks brief. The choirs led the throng of festival goers with a spiritual, soulful, impacting rendition of "Down in the Valley." The crowd dispersed. The first Remembrance of Good Days Past—We Have Time for You festival was history.

Again the mayor thought he spotted that shaggy white-haired man with the scraggly long beard dressed in bib overalls, hunched over with a seemingly random indifferent demeanor, following him throughout the parade route and again popping out from behind a large maple tree in the park during the closing ceremony. *Oh well*, thought the mayor—*I must be seeing apparitions. I'm totally exhausted, beyond tired. I've got to get some well-deserved sleep.* And off he went home to recall these past few days and give himself a pat on the back for being the engine that helped put this entire gigantic effort together.

He would meet in a week or so to review the event with his board, but now well-deserved shut-eye awaited.

The Story Ends

And Life in Richville Goes On

The week after the festival, Cooky, at home with hospice care, lie dying, his demeanor calm, his breathing, however, weak. His family physician had come and gone, prescribing some pain medication. Reverend Huether visited and gave a blessing. Nelly allowed no other visitors other than the immediate family.

Nelly entered the darkened room, the spare bedroom with shades drawn, one small lamp lighting the room.

"You know we have had a great life together— working, playing, raising a family, taking care of this town's eating habits. I love you more than you can possibly know," she choked out.

"Remember that cameo broach you gave me on our first anniversary, your great-grandmother's that was lost a few years later? Don't talk, Cooky. Well, I found it of all places on the kitchen windowsill. How very strange. Remember, our house had been broken into way, way back. I don't know. Maybe it was stolen; maybe someone did return it. How very strange," she lamented.

She placed the broach in Cooky's hand. He clutched it and looked up at Nelly. His breathing became fainter and fainter. With a final sigh he took his last breath.

Word got around town that items that were missing from families, stolen or lost, were being returned. A grandfather clock that belonged to the Gobbel family was unceremoniously propped up against their barn.

The Carlotto family had an expensive diamond studded dinner plate with the date of the founding of their rock business printed in gold leaf returned to their warehouse. Someone would have had to break in over a weekend to carefully place this artifact on a workbench inside the warehouse.

The Knudson family had a family album of historic pictures from Sweden returned dumped one night on their doorstep.

And on and on went the strange events in which valuable artifacts were returned to their rightful owners.

The rumors flew around as to who had these items in the first place. It seemed to be random acts, but the conclusion was that probably one person was responsible.

But, again, why would anyone want to confront this individual if indeed it was this specific person. Most of Richville's residents, as they tended to do when thinking collectively, just "let it pass—no harm, no foul."

The mayor, collecting his strength having rested for a week after the festival, now sat alone in his office at the administration building.

He glanced at a sign on the wall he referred to when times were tough; he had this poem memorized, but now he studied it word by word:

> Don't promise anything unless you
> mean the word you say. Don't break
> your pledge to anyone, tomorrow or
> today because a promise is no thing
> you can toss aside. Indeed it is a solemn
> bond too difficult to hide. Of course you

can be reckless and indifferent as can
be. And maybe you're not interested in
downright honesty. But if you want to
earn respect and be of some good worth
fulfill the smallest promise that you make
upon this earth. It is much better never
to declare a wow at all than to express
assurance you care not to recall."

There was not much more time for reflection, as the
problems of the day in Richville would need attending. The
growth of this town now 5,262 as of 12:00 PM this day in
September needed answers for the community concerns of
police and fire protection, a better infrastructure, maintenance
and expansion of the park system, more opportunities for
youth involvement, and a better business climate to induce
people to come to this rural midwestern town to plant roots
and become good citizens, helping each other in a spirit of
cooperation and free enterprise.

The mayor further reflected, *This town must remain
true to its identity, not grow out of proportion with its values
and soul. Don't sell out to the big corporate entities beginning
to dot the landscape around Richville. Be true to traditions
and family values.*

He sighed and now said to himself—"I'm again ready
to tackle those community concerns along with the council
and our new city manager Myron Proudfoot."

The citizens and business owners who have stayed in
Richville to put down those roots to build their businesses
and families have been rewarded with lives of enrichment and
blessings beyond the financial gain.

Overall, the motivations of the citizens of Richville have been pure and straight-forward, each lending their unique style and strength to the fabric of the community.

A new era is coming to Richville, one filled with complex challenges needing the entire community's attention and resolve.

This first community festival Remembrance of Good Days Past—Richville Has Time For You is a start toward allowing all community members to engage their own unique talents and skills toward preserving the traditions from the previous generations and starting new traditions to lead into the future.

Even citizens who may not have been previously engaged in this most communal of activities may eventually become involved in future endeavors related to this growing festival.

Remember, Richville, this small rural midwestern town in mid America has time for you.

And life goes on in Richville.

Postscript

Youth Will Be Served

The ten-year-old had taken it all in from that first meeting of the town's notables at Cooky's Café to the end of the parade and the post-festival examination of what went right, what went wrong, and what would be changed or altered if, indeed, there was to be a second Remembrance of Good Days Past.

This youth gained an appreciation for the quaint adults in his life who paraded their many skills in a unified effort to put together some sort of cohesive plan that would culminate in the greater good for all the citizens of this small rural community.

What seemed to him to be just wordy pronouncements at first turned into planning and implementation of these words into noble deeds, which thrilled him, at least as much as could infect a ten year old who, as yet, was not really a part of the movement of this, to him, bigger-than-life event.

Like pieces of a puzzle, in this youth's mind he saw fragments of the whole. The human element always in the forefront with is frailties, often misconceptions, selfish behavior, even a mundane decision, which, in fact, may have been the one decisive result leading to the capstone and final piece of the puzzle. This youth took these perceptions, sorted them out, and discovered the elements of truth he would need in his future endeavors, keeping this completed puzzle intact.

Each day's occurrences for this youth added to a foundation that would not be tarnished or broken. Like other youth who lived in Richville, the surface experiences were taken somewhat for granted—the day-to-day schooling, the after school and weekend activities, the innocent and not-so-innocent trouble these youth could find, the select friends bound together by an oath not to be cast aside. Each assorted group vowed allegiance to each other and an abhorrence to these foreign beings in other towns and provinces in other faraway lands.

As a ten year old, this youth was buoyed by his close-knit and extended family, their love providing him with sustenance and warmth especially on those much-needed spiritual cold days when the fortunes of change and confusion faced this youth and seemed to threaten his very existence.

He gained an appreciation for the diversity of citizenry in his rural dwelling. *How could,* he remarked to himself, *there be so many people with so many different opinions about the day-to-day life here in Richville, yet be similar in so many respects?*

He slowly discovered that not all commerce represented just an exchange of tokens to purchase items of need and want, but commerce also represented an intermingling of joy, sorrow, concern for others, and a sense of pride building on pride, which led to a profound sense of a community's self-worth and good standing in the region.

Each year after this initial awakening, this youth would gain a further understanding of his role in this complicated process of leadership.

After all, it was his father, the mayor of Richville, who initiated this grand design and left the process to others to continue this fine tradition into the unknown future.

This ten year old took the leadership role and, undaunted, stayed to complete that which could never really be completed—a continuing saga of life's struggles to maintain those early traditions and to continue to add to the rich fabric of this community's life blood—a festival unlike any other in the region.

As the last of the parade's floats, the classic cars and one slime green monster truck, drifted by the Flamingo Grill on Main Street of this rustic rural community of Richville, the sixty-year-old son of the deceased mayor stood fixed in front of the grill and breathed a sigh of relief, for another festival was complete, the fiftieth, another enriching four days where again this community had come together to celebrate its many traditions for all the region to witness and experience.

And life goes on in Richville, a town that always has time for you.

Only the beginning...

Addendum

Blue ribbon winners of the Jams, Jellies and Preserves contest

The contest rules separated the categories into what constitutes a jam, a jelly, and a preserve.

1. Jam is a thick mixture of fruit, pectin, and sugar that is boiled gently but quickly until the fruit is soft and has an organic shape yet is still thick enough that it spreads easily and can form a blob; jams are also good for fillings.

2. Jelly is made from sugar, pectin, acid, and fruit juice and is a clear spread that is firm enough to hold its shape. Jellies can be made from ingredients other than fruit such as herbs, tea, wine, liquors, flowers, and vegetables.

3. Preserves are spreads that have chunks of fruit surrounded by jelly.

Blue Ribbon Jam
entered by Margerie McQuade (Jam Pot special)

900 g fruit (blackberries, plums, raspberries, strawberries)
900 g golden granulated sugar
Knob of butter

1. Put fruit into a preserving pan or heavy based saucepan. For blackberries, add 50 ml of water and 1 ½ tbsp of lemon juice; for plums (halved and stoned), use 150 ml of water; for strawberries add 3 tbsp of lemon juice (no water); and for raspberries add nothing. Bring to a boil.

2. Lower the heat. For blackberries, simmer for 15 minutes; for plums simmer for 30–40 minutes; for raspberries simmer for two minutes; for strawberries simmer for five minutes. The fruit should be soft.

3. Trip in the sugar and stir over a very low heat until the sugar has completely dissolved. Raise the heat, bring to a rolling boil, then rapidly boil blackberries for 10–12 minutes, plums for 10 minutes, raspberries for 5 minutes, or strawberries for 20–25 minutes—don't stir though until the setting point of 105° C is reached.

4. Remove from heat, skim off any excess scum, then stir a knob of butter across the surface (this helps to dissolve any remaining scum). Leave for about 15 minutes so the fruit can settle. Pour into sterilized jars, label, and seal.

Blue Ribbon Jelly

entered by Aunt Flora Snodgrass (rhubarb/cherry delight)
The jelly good for the belly

6 cups diced rhubarb
4 cups white sugar
1 (21 ounce) can cherry pie filling
1 (6 ounce) package cherry flavored Jello

1. Place rhubarb in a large bowl. Pour sugar over top and stir to coat. Cover bowl and refrigerate overnight.

2. Place rhubarb mixture in a pot and cook over medium heat until tender, stirring frequently. Stir in pie filling and gelatin and bring mixture to a boil. Pour into a shallow pan and allow to cool in refrigerator. When jelly is cool, pack into jars or plastic containers. Can be refrigerated or frozen.

Blue Ribbon Preserve
entered by Adelaide Gobbel
(watermelon rind preserve par excellence)

4 pounds chopped watermelon rind
1 gallon water
½ cup salt
9 cups white sugar
8 cups water
4 teaspoons crushed cinnamon stick
4 teaspoons ground cloves
4 lemons—rinsed, sliced, and seeded
1 dash red food coloring

1. Peel off the green part of the watermelon rind and slice into
   2 inch pieces. Soak the rind in a solution of 1 gallon water
   and ½ cup salt overnight.

2. Remove rind from salt water and place in a stock pot with
   clean water to cover. Bring to a boil over medium high heat
   and cook for about 30 minutes or until rind is tender. Drain.

3. In a large pot, combine the sugar, 8 cups water, and sliced
   lemons. Tie the cinnamon and cloves into a cheesecloth bag
   and place in the pot. Bring the syrup to a boil and boil for 5
   minutes, Add the rinds and cook until transparent. Remove
   spice bag. Stir in red food coloring. Ladle preserves into
   hot sterile jars and process to seal.

Raccoon Kabobs

*submitted at the first Remembrance of Good Days Past
festival by Bud (Wheels) Wheeler
(original founding member of the Richville "Thank
Goodness I'm Alive and Kicking" Club)*

2 pounds fresh raccoon meat—cut into one inch cubes
½ cup homemade French dressing
2 green peppers, cut into squares
1 onion—cut into squares
⅓ pound mushroom caps

1. Place raccoon cubes in a ceramic bowl. Pour dressing over cubes and marinate for 2 to 3 hours.

2. Remove cubes, reserve marinade.

3. On skewers, alternate raccoon pieces with pepper squares, onion pieces, and mushroom caps, brushing everything with reserved marinade.

4. Broil over hot coals until done, turning frequently and basting with marinade as needed.

This recipe led to the festival adding many road-kill recipes over succeeding years, thanks to the dogged determination of Bud (Wheels) Wheeler.

our rural small town friend lives in all our hearts.

Same time and place next month

By BOB JONES

His work shed was attached to the back of the garage; a handmade 12-by-10-foot knotty pine enclosed room with a workbench; hooks on the wall for hand tools; various styles, sizes and shapes of golf clubs stashed in a corner (he was in the golf club design business for many years).

On a table beside the workbench was his team's track trophy won 25 years previous; a regional championship.

Modern amenities languished in this den most primal - a flat-screen TV, a small refrigerator housed various liquid drinks; two ornately colored beach chairs were placed across from the workbench; a halogen lamp shone brightly, casting uneven light throughout the room.

Objects were strewn about randomly, albeit clumped together in some semi-organized fashion - fishing lures and plugs, fishing reels with knotted lines and poles placed upright with no particular sense of direction.

A litter box with cat chow next to it was on the floor next to the door. A feral feline sauntered in and out throughout my stay - seeming uninterested at my presence, but knowing my whereabouts at all times.

Once a month my friend and I passed the time spinning yarns to each other, settling world and domestic disputes, catching up on life's joys and serene moments of peace, and forgetting for the moment life's woes and ailing troubles.

"No more golf," my friend states. "Back too strained, heel permanently bruised, eyesight bad, motivation lacking."

"We are lucky to be in this moment," I say. "Alive, still kicking, having spouses who still for whatever reason love us, and grandchildren who we adore. Life is good."

My friend changes direction: "No gardening this season for me. Too many bugs and floods. My tomato plants washed out last season."

"I'll stick with perennials and wildflowers, and just maintaining a healthy lawn," I say.

"Any plans to travel?" I ask.

"Nope," comes a terse response.

"Same time and place next month," I say instinctively, feeling the hours passing.

"Call me," comes the response.

I leave knowing business has been duly conducted, the gavel has been pounded for this meeting to end.

I would call about our next month's meeting. A new yet continuing agenda would be on the table.

Friendships like this endure until "death do us part." In this homemade room, my friend and I have shared our life stories over the years.

I bid adieu to my friend and part company. Same time and place next month. Goodbye old friend.

Bob Jones is a resident of Washington Township.

Very First U.S. Silver Dollar Ever Minted!

Buy the book, *Birth of a Tradition: Tales and Travails from Rural Richville—A Place That Has Time for You*, and enter your name, phone, and/or email address to rmjones@ provide.net for a chance to win a replica .999 silver wt. .71 mg., 39mm diameter, individually struck proof replica of the first US Silver dollar. Two winners will be notified in October 2016.

In book two, *Another Tale of Travail and Treachery in Richville: The Underbelly Exposed*, feuding families pursue this gem and a prized Paul Revere teapot to claim their supposed fame and fortune.

The underbelly of this small rural community is exposed for all to see with dismay and dishonor.

Proceeds from the sale of the book beyond publishing costs go to support the fine and performing arts (Top Tier Entertainment).

Looking North Up Main Street

Another View of Main Street

Main Street Heading Toward Billings Gate Park

The Original Carlotto Family Home

The Pristine Nature of the Family Farm

Richville Garden Club Members Plan Their Part for the Festival

The Massive Richville Catholic Church
Planned and Built by the Carlotto Family

Vast Undeveloped Land Behind the Gobbel Farm

*The Implement of Choice for Many Generations
of Richville Farmers*

Mayor Mervin Leroy
A Testament to Determination and Political Know-How
A Job Well Done

CPSIA information can be obtained
at www.ICGtesting.com
Printed in the USA
FFOW05n0054260716

9 781608 805242